"Lying here next to you after all this time makes me wish I'd gotten one last kiss before I let you go. I regret that more than anything else."

Without thinking, Harley surged forward and his lips pressed to hers. He'd had those regrets, too, and now, having her so near, he couldn't fight it anymore. He had to touch her, taste her, even if it was just to convince himself that his memories of her were wrong. She couldn't possibly be everything he'd built her up to be in his mind. She'd become a fantasy he couldn't have. He hoped that once the kiss was done he could put aside his attraction to her and focus on the case.

He couldn't have been more wrong. Jade melted into his arms, moaning softly against his mouth. She wrapped her body around him, pulling him close.

There was no going back.

She was everything he remembered and more.

* * *

From Mistake to Millions is the first book of the Switched! duet.

Dear Reader,

As much as I've loved hanging out in the Millionaires of Manhattan world for the last year or so, it was time to start something new! Don't worry, that series will continue at some point, but I decided it was time to trade in the hustle and bustle of New York for the sultry Southern style of Charleston.

The idea for this new series started with all those commercials for DNA testing kits on television. I thought that was going to dig up some skeletons, for sure. And that's where Switched! begins. Jade Nolan has only ever wanted a happy, ordinary life, always striving for quiet and simple pleasures. Her first love, bad boy Harley Dalton, never fit into those tidy plans. She made the tough choice to leave him behind, only to find him back on her doorstep more than ten years later. She can't turn away from him now if she wants to get to the truth about her family. And to be honest, there's no way she can walk away from this sexy chapter from her past.

If you enjoy Jade and Harley's story, tell me by visiting my website at andrealaurence.com, liking my fan page on Facebook or following me on Twitter or Instagram. I'd love to hear from you!

Enjoy,

Andrea

ANDREA LAURENCE

FROM MISTAKE TO MILLIONS

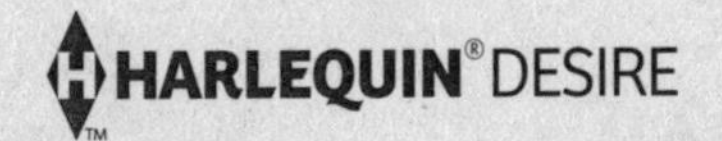

ISBN-13: 978-1-335-60371-5

From Mistake to Millions

This edition published by arrangement with Harlequin Books S.A.

For questions and comments about the quality of this book, please contact us at CustomerService@Harlequin.com.

Printed in U.S.A.

Andrea Laurence is an award-winning author of contemporary romances filled with seduction and sass. She has been a lover of reading and writing stories since she was young. A dedicated West Coast girl transplanted into the Deep South, she is thrilled to share her special blend of sensuality and dry, sarcastic humor with readers.

Books by Andrea Laurence

Harlequin Desire

Millionaires of Manhattan

What Lies Beneath
More Than He Expected
His Lover's Little Secret
The CEO's Unexpected Child
Little Secrets: Secretly Pregnant
Rags to Riches Baby
One Unforgettable Weekend
The Boyfriend Arrangement

Switched!

From Mistake to Millions

Visit her Author Profile page at Harlequin.com, or andrealaurence.com, for more titles.

You can find Andrea Laurence on Facebook, along with other Harlequin Desire authors, at Facebook.com/harlequindesireauthors!

Prologue

This couldn't be right.

Jade Nolan studied the genetic test report she'd just received in the mail. The DNA kit had been a Christmas gift from her younger brother, Dean. He'd gotten it for everyone in the family this year. He thought it would be fun to see what parts of the world they'd come from. They were fairly certain of the family's Irish and German heritage, so there weren't going to be many surprises.

But the words Jade was looking at were a surprise and then some. They were actually a shock.

"Jade? Are you okay?"

She looked up from the paper in her hand and stared blankly at her best friend, Sophie Kane.

They were hanging out drinking wine and watching their favorite show together just like they did every Tuesday. But the minute Jade looked at the report, the evening had taken a sharp, unexpected turn.

"No," she said with a shake of her head. "I'm not okay."

How could she be okay? According to the report, she wasn't closely related to any other users in the company's database. Considering that she'd been the last of her family to mail in her DNA sample, that wasn't possible. Both her parents and her brother had submitted their DNA weeks before she had. They should be showing under the family section of her report. And yet they weren't.

Never mind the fact that her DNA showed she wasn't Irish and German. She was coming up English, Swedish and Dutch. She'd seen her brother's report and they didn't align at all.

"What does it say?" Sophie pressed. She set down her wine and leaned in to lay a comforting hand on Jade's shoulder. "Tell me, honey."

Jade swallowed hard, trying to dislodge the lump that had suddenly formed in her throat. She couldn't speak. In an instant, a lifetime of unfounded doubts had rushed into her mind. Years of being the family misfit. Insecurity about her physical differences. Jokes about being the milkman's daughter, since she was blonde with dark brown eyes, and the rest of her family had dark, almost black hair and green eyes. The jokes were all too real now.

No matter how many times her mother had assured her that her grandmother was a blonde, no matter how many grainy old pictures were hauled out to prove that her willow-thin frame came from her father's family, it didn't help. Her grandmother's hair had been a dishwater blond in her youth, not Jade's pale, almost platinum color. The family in the old pictures were poor and undernourished, not naturally slim like Jade, with her ballerina's body.

Jade had always felt like the odd one out. Now she had the cold, hard evidence to prove what she'd known all along. She was not a Nolan.

She stood up suddenly and the report slipped from her fingers, falling to the floor. Jade didn't notice.

"I think I'm...*adopted*." She was finally able to say the words aloud, but they sounded foreign to her ears.

Adopted. The reality of it was like a fist to the gut. Why had her parents kept this from her? She was almost thirty years old. She had married and divorced. When she and her ex-husband, Lance, were discussing children, her mother had even told her stories about her pregnancy with Jade. About how her father had fainted in the delivery room. Now Jade realized it was all a lie. An elaborate, complicated lie.

But why?

She didn't understand what was going on. But she would get to the bottom of it one way or another.

One

Being the boss was boring as hell.

Harley Dalton sat on the top floor of his Washington, DC, office building and flipped through some reports. He wasn't reading them. Managing a company wasn't really his thing. He'd started one only because he didn't want to take orders again after getting out of the navy.

He'd never expected it to be so successful. Dalton Security now had four offices in the US and one in London, with hundreds of employees. They were the company to call if you found yourself in a bind, or if a situation needed to be handled. Nothing outright illegal, of course, but things would be dealt with in a quick and efficient manner that sometimes fell into a fuzzy gray area.

One of the things his company had handled was the recent abduction of a fourteen-year-old girl. She'd run away with her soccer coach, who was nearly fifty. It was on the nationwide news as people hunted for the young girl across the Midwest. It was also on the news when Dalton Security successfully tracked down, apprehended and delivered the pervert who'd kidnapped her to the front door of the police station, a little worse for wear. The girl was returned home safely. Dalton's stock prices had shot through the roof. All ended well.

At least well enough, considering Harley found himself in stuffy suits sitting at big desks talking to people all day. He wasn't the one in the field anymore and it grated on him. He wasn't toting a Glock and apprehending suspects. He was a damn paper pusher now.

He'd never imagined that being a millionaire would suck so hard.

"Mr. Dalton?" His assistant's voice chimed over the intercom on his phone.

"Yes?" he replied, trying not to growl at Faye. It wasn't her fault he was feeling strangled by his silk tie today.

"I have a Mr. Jeffries on the phone, sir."

Jeffries? The name didn't sound familiar. "Who is he?"

"He says he's the CEO of St. Francis Hospital in Charleston."

Now why would the CEO of a Charleston hospital be calling him? Harley had been born and raised in the city, but hadn't been back in a decade. His mother still lived there. He'd bought her a beautiful old plantation house that he had yet to visit. The CEO wouldn't be calling if something had happened to his mother. What could it be? Normally Harley didn't take phone calls from people he didn't know, but his curiosity was piqued.

"Put him through," he told Faye.

The phone chimed a moment later and he picked up. "This is Dalton," he said.

"Hello. This is Weston Jeffries. I'm the CEO of the St. Francis Hospital group in Charleston. I was hoping to speak with you about a...*situation* we're having here."

"Normally new cases are handled by our client intake department," Harley said. If they wanted special surveillance equipment or needed to investigate pending hires, that didn't need to come across his desk.

"I understand that," Mr. Jeffries said. "But from one CEO to another, this is a really delicate situation for us. We've already gotten more media scrutiny than we care to."

Media scrutiny? Apparently he needed to pay more attention to what was going on back home.

"Well, why don't you tell me what's happening and I'll see what we can do."

"We've been contacted by a woman who claims she was switched at birth when she was born at our hospital here in 1989. She'd thought at first maybe she'd been adopted, but her parents are adamant that they delivered a daughter at St. Francis that day. She believes them, so in her mind, that only leaves the possibility that she was switched as an infant here. We are looking for someone to investigate what happened, as quietly as possible. The woman has already gone to the local news and we don't want to make the situation worse than it already is."

While someone being switched at birth was interesting and potentially damaging to the hospital, he still wasn't sure why the man insisted on speaking to him about it. Then again, Harley was bored to tears. He might as well listen. "Do you believe the hospital was at fault?"

"It's hard to say. Our technology and security weren't as good back then as they are now. The woman was also born in the middle of Hurricane Hugo, so it wasn't exactly business as usual around the hospital at that time."

Hurricane Hugo? That was an odd coincidence. His girlfriend back in high school had been born during Hurricane Hugo. His mind was suddenly flooded with memories of the willowy blonde who had headlined his teenage fantasies. She had been beautiful, smart and way out of his league. After she'd dumped him, he'd tried to put the memory of her in the past where it belonged, but he found that thoughts of her crept into his mind more often than he liked.

Like now.

He wasn't listening to a word the man was saying. "What was the woman's name?" he interrupted.

"Jade Nolan."

Upon hearing her name, Harley felt as if someone had reached out and punched him in the gut. Jade. Of all the women in Charleston, it had to be her case that dropped in his lap. Against his better judgment, he knew in that moment that his company would take the case. He also knew that for the first time in several years, he was going to handle it personally.

It might not be the healthiest thing to do, emotionally, but he had to see her again. It had been almost twelve years since she'd broken up with him and run off with that insipid little weasel, Lance Rhodes. He'd heard that she'd married him. Maybe she was still married to him. He'd seemed to be everything she wanted. Everything Harley wasn't.

Call it morbid curiosity. Call it a reason to get out of this office with the walls closing in on him like a Star Wars trash compactor. But he was driving to Charleston in the morning.

"Mr. Dalton?"

Harley again realized he'd been sitting silently on the line for too long. "I'm sorry, Mr. Jeffries. We'll take the case. Someone will be calling you back to get more details, but I will be down in Charleston within the week."

"You're going to handle it personally?"

"In this situation, yes."

"Thank you so much, Mr. Dalton. I look forward to speaking to you when you come into town."

The call ended and Harley sat back in his chair to consider the ramifications of what he'd just done. Taking the case on wasn't the problem. He had no doubt that his team would uncover the truth of what had happened, if anything had happened at all. Going down personally was another matter. He could tell himself it was a good excuse to visit his mother and see his old stomping grounds, but anyone who knew him back then would know that he was going down there to see Jade.

She wasn't the right kind of girl for him. He'd known that back in high school. He'd spent a lot of time in detention, while she was the treasurer of the National Honor Society. They ran in completely different social circles—Jade with the smart kids and him with the juvenile delinquents. And yet the first moment he'd laid eyes on her in their French class, he knew he was done for.

Maybe it was those big Bambi eyes that stood out against her pale skin and ice-blond hair. Even now, he remembered what it felt like to rub those silky strands between his fingers. She'd always looked at him with a touch of curiosity and anxiety hidden beneath thick lashes. The anxiety he was used to; he'd had quite the reputation around their high school. It was the curiosity that intrigued him.

Although he was doing fine in French, he'd pretended he wasn't and had approached her about tutoring him after school for some extra cash. He knew her family didn't have a lot of money. Neither did he, but he was willing to part with what little he had to spend some time with her.

Harley had paid her ten dollars a week for the rest of the semester to sit with him and practice French. He'd ended up getting an A in the class, which wasn't his goal, but it hadn't hurt. He'd just wanted to spend time with Jade, and he didn't think she would do it otherwise. He was wrong. One sultry summer night in Charleston, he'd worked up the nerve to kiss her, and everything had changed. Including him.

He had spent most of his youth running wild. His mother, a single mom, had worked two jobs to keep them afloat, so he'd spent most of his time without adult supervision. When he was with Jade, his usual pastimes didn't seem as exciting anymore. He'd found he much preferred the rush of kissing her, or nearly being caught by her parents when he'd sneak in through her bedroom window at night. She was everything he hadn't thought he would want. His previous romantic experiences had involved girls with too much makeup and too much time on their hands.

Jade thought about nothing but the future. She'd been so desperate to avoid the struggles of her parents that she was constantly worried about her grades, which college she might get into and what she was going to do with her life. He had no doubt that one day she would be Dr. Jade Nolan.

What Harley wasn't so sure about was how he might fit into Jade's future. Apparently, she had the same concerns. Not long after she'd started college, she broke things off with him. He knew as well as anybody that they weren't right for each other—or more accurately, that he wasn't good enough for her. So he hadn't fought to keep her. That was one of his biggest regrets, if he admitted to any at all. He preferred to look forward. And that's what he'd done.

A week later, he'd walked into the navy recruiting office and never looked back. He hadn't seen Jade since that day they broke up, despite her being on his mind all the time.

Glancing down now at the information he'd copied into his notebook during the call, he figured that was all about to change.

The doorbell rang.

Jade knew the investigator the hospital had hired

was coming to interview her today, so she leaped up from the couch when she heard the chime ring through the house. Someone from St. Francis had called to make sure she would be home. She wasn't entirely sure what she would tell the investigator, since she'd been literally just born at the time the incident took place, but at the very least, she could get an idea of who this person was and how he or she would handle things.

The company had been hired by the hospital, after all. Her best friend and pro bono attorney, Sophie, had given her sound advice. She'd suggested they go to the local media when the hospital had tried to brush her off. Within twenty-four hours of her interview with the press, the hospital's legal team had phoned and told her they were hiring a third-party investigator to determine what had happened. Apparently they'd gotten a lot of flak, especially when the news station contacted them and they refused to comment.

That was a week ago. Things had changed quickly.

Jade went to answer the door, flinging it open in a rush, and then stopping short as she recognized the man standing on her porch. In an instant, her heart stuttered, her body stiffened. It was like she'd run straight into a brick wall she hadn't seen coming.

"Hello, Jade."

There was no way she could've seen *this* coming. Her mouth dropped open, the words dying on her lips. She couldn't even manage to say hello. Not with her ex-boyfriend Harley Dalton standing on her front porch.

It had been forever since she'd seen him—her first semester of college, to be precise. A lot had changed about Harley since then. He was bigger now. Brawny, almost. She'd heard that he went into the navy after they'd broken up, and it showed as his broad shoulders strained against his expensive, tailored gray suit coat. He'd dwarfed her in high school and there was an even more pronounced size difference between them now.

A lot of things were still the same, however. The dark blue eyes with the wicked glint. The broken nose. The devilish smile that promised more than she could handle, then or now…

The way he looked at her was different, though. The heat in his eyes wasn't stoked by desire today. It felt more like animosity. And close scrutiny. It was startling to see that, although Jade supposed he might still be mad at her for breaking up with him all those years ago.

"Jade?" He arched a brow, a questioning look on his face.

She clamped her jaw shut and nodded. "Hello, Harley," she finally managed to say. "Sorry."

"So you *do* remember me," he said with a smirk.

As though she was ever likely to forget. He'd

been her first love. Maybe her only real love, if she was honest with herself. She wasn't about to let him know that. "Of course I remember you. What are you doing here?"

"St. Francis hired me—my company, rather—to look into your claims of staff misconduct at the hospital."

Jade hadn't kept tabs on Harley over the years, but that type of work seemed right up his alley. Maybe if she had paid more attention, she wouldn't have been blindsided when the hospital hired him—the one man she'd managed to avoid successfully all these years. "Oh," she said, trying not to sound disappointed or concerned. There wasn't much she could do about it now. Even if she called the hospital and complained later, it wouldn't get Harley Dalton off her front porch today.

"They didn't tell me who to expect. I didn't realize… Come in," she offered, taking a step back from the door to let him inside her small rental house.

As he stepped over the threshold, the faint breeze blew in with him and brought the scent of him to her nose. The woodsy fragrance of his cologne mingled with his familiar manly musk immediately took her back to being eighteen again. To snuggling against him in his pickup truck. To fogging up the windows while he nibbled on her neck…

Whatever confidence and self-assurance she'd gained over the years faded to nothing when she looked at him. In their place was a flutter of butterflies in her stomach and a sudden awareness of parts of her body that she hadn't noticed in a very long time. Maybe since the last time she'd touched Harley. Lance had been a lot of things, but an intensely sexual creature was not one of them.

Jade had been okay with that. She'd traded that intense passion for security and stability. Or so she'd thought. Being around Harley again had just reminded her of everything she'd passed up in her quest for a better life.

It was a high price to pay. She'd been in the same room with him for less than a minute now and was already almost overwhelmed by his presence. She needed a moment alone or wasn't sure she could get through a half hour interview without making a fool of herself.

"Would you like something to drink? Some sweet tea?" she asked.

"Sure. Thank you."

Jade gestured toward the couch. "Have a seat. I'll be right back."

She immediately turned on her heel and disappeared into the kitchen, trying to erase from her mind the image of him smiling at her. At one time, she'd lamented the closed-off floor plan of the older home she was renting, but now was relieved to have a barrier of wood and drywall between them.

Jade took her time pouring two glasses of sweet

tea, and even put together a plate of cookies. She remembered that Harley had a sweet tooth, and that bought her a few more seconds to compose herself. But eventually she had to go back to the living room and face him again.

She wasn't sure what to think of his sudden appearance, or the faint scowl on his face. Questions were swirling through her mind. Did he not believe her side of the story about being switched? He had been hired by the hospital, after all. Or was it because he was still angry with her? If so, why had he taken the case? Was it because he still found her attractive? If so, did she really care? She wasn't really equipped to deal with something like that right now, what with everything else in her life spinning out of control.

"Do you need any help?"

Jade jerked her head up and saw Harley peeking around the corner. Trying not to look startled, she took the plate of cookies and handed it to him. "Here, take these. I'll carry the tea."

"Mmm, shortbread," he said, appreciation lighting his eyes.

"Those were your favorites, weren't they?" she asked, wishing immediately that she hadn't. She didn't want him to think she recalled things like that after all these years apart.

"They still are. I can't believe you remember." Harley popped a cookie into his mouth and chewed thoughtfully, drawing Jade's attention to his full lips.

A lot of time had passed, and yet it felt like almost none at all when she looked at Harley. She could almost feel those lips on hers as if it was yesterday. He might have been a bad boy, but he was a good kisser. A great one.

How long had it been since Jade had been kissed?

A real kiss. Not a peck. A long, slow, toe-curling kiss? She didn't even know. A long time. Sadly, it had been long before her husband turned away from her and had taken up drugs instead.

Deep inside, a part of her wished to experience that thrill of attraction again. To feel wanted and desired. But she knew that Harley was not the one to relight those fires. Those flames would be all consuming and that was a risk she wasn't willing to take. Not back then and not now.

Harley finished his cookie and smiled at her in a way that made her wonder if he knew exactly what she was thinking. Jade had never been very good at hiding her emotions, but she needed to do better. Especially when he was around. He was here to interview her about her claims against the hospital, but she could just as easily be a teenager again, helping him study French over tea and cookies, and fantasizing about making it to second base.

He turned and walked into the living room, and with no other choice, she followed him. Harley sat on the end of the couch and she opted for the chair to his right. She set the tea on the table, unsure of how to start this conversation. Did they go straight to the investigation and ignore the elephant in the room? Or should they take the time to catch up after more than a decade of not seeing each other?

"So how have you been?" he asked, making the decision for her.

"Good," she said on reflex. Since her divorce, people were always asking her how she was. She found they didn't really want to hear the truth. "Most days, at least. A lot has changed since I saw you last, but I'm doing okay."

Harley glanced down at her hand and his brows knitted together in confusion. Presumably he was looking for the wedding ring she'd taken off a long time ago. "I heard you married Lance, but I don't see a ring."

"I did marry him. My junior year of college," Jade said. "It ended a couple years ago."

Harley straightened, apparently unaware of what had happened. She was surprised the investigator hadn't thoroughly looked into her past before he'd arrived. "I'm sorry to hear that," he said.

Jade could only nod. She didn't want to tell him about what had happened with Lance. It wasn't a pretty story, but it had been in the news and anyone with a desire to could look it up. He could get all the details if he wanted to know.

"What about you? Any family?"

Harley chuckled and shook his head. “Oh, no. I spent eight years in the navy, traveling all over the world. There wasn’t much time for starting a family or even settling down in one spot. After I got out, I started my own business. That takes up every moment of your day for a while. Thankfully, things are running smoothly, without my constant supervision, now.”

Jade hadn’t been sure what Harley would do with his life. Some had bet their money he’d end up in jail. Others, that he’d accomplish nothing. She had seen more potential in him than that, and was pleased to hear he’d become an entrepreneur.

“So your company does private investigations? Like hired detectives?”

“Not entirely. Across our five locations, we do a lot of different work that falls in the security detail bucket. Personal security and protection, home security setup and monitoring, missing persons cases…lots of different things where the police can’t or won’t step in, for whatever reason. We specialize in government contracts and a higher end clientele who want to keep things quiet. Investigations are just one aspect of what we do at Dalton Security.”

Dalton Security? Now that he’d said it, Jade realized she’d heard of the company. Maybe in reference to the recent Bennett kidnapping case. That had been on every news channel she’d seen for weeks.

Dalton Security had broken the case wide open and delivered the teen back to her parents.

It had never occurred to her that it was Harley's business. It sounded like he was doing even better for himself than she had hoped. The nice suit and gold Rolex on his wrist were evidence enough of that. She was glad to hear it. Jade knew his mother had struggled to raise him on her own. The last she remembered, Harley's mom had worked as a cashier at a grocery store and cleaned houses on the side.

"This seems like a pretty puny job in the scheme of things your company handles. Why would the CEO of Dalton Security—of all people—be working a case like this?"

Harley's gaze met hers and she felt a shiver run through her whole body. When he looked at her that way, it was as though he could see straight through her, into her soul. There was nothing she could hide from him. She was an open book left out for him to read if he wanted to bother. It was unnerving and thrilling at the same time. For so long, she'd felt invisible.

Harley saw her.

"Isn't that obvious, Jade? I took the case so I could see you again."

Two

The sight of Jade was breathtaking.

Damn it.

Harley hadn't known what to expect when he walked up to her door. She had been a pretty teenager. Pretty enough to headline in every one of his high school fantasies, and a couple of his grown-up ones. A part of him had hoped that she wouldn't be as attractive as he remembered. That perhaps she'd aged poorly or had taken up chain smoking. That would make it easier for him to do his job and walk away from the whole situation as planned.

But when she opened her front door today…he had to brace himself for the impact of how stunningly beautiful a woman she'd become. She still had the kind of naturally platinum blond hair that women spent a fortune on in the salon. It was just pulled back into a sleek ponytail, but the ringlets that fell down her neck were captivating. With her pale complexion and large eyes, she was like a flawless porcelain doll.

It was an incredibly frustrating sight for Harley, making the situation infinitely more complicated. Curiosity and boredom had brought him to Jade's door. Her beauty could keep him around longer than was necessary to wrap up this case. He was painfully aware that the attraction between the two of them was just as intense as it ever was. The look in her eyes when she marched off into the kitchen told him that much.

To be honest, that was the last thing he wanted to know. Being attracted to Jade hadn't ended well for him the first time. Not because it wasn't reciprocal; he could've taken that. No, his heartburn came from the fact that even though she'd wanted Harley, she'd chosen Lance. That spoke volumes. Just because her ex wasn't in the picture any longer didn't mean anything had changed. She might still prefer a stuffed shirt over a guy like Harley. Fate had brought them back together, but it didn't mean this time would be any different for the two of them.

And yet the way that Jade had looked at him when he said he was here to see her made him realize she had no clue how beautiful she truly was, or how he could still be attracted to her after all this time. That was a damned shame. What had happened to her since the last time he saw her that she could ever doubt it? What had her suitable, respectable husband done to break Jade's spirit?

"You took the case just to see me?" she asked in obvious confusion and doubt. Jade seemed baffled by the whole situation. In fairness, he'd had several days to prepare to see her again, and she'd been thrown a curveball without warning.

"Let me rephrase that." He backtracked, realizing the implications of his words. "I wanted to make sure your case was handled by the best guy at my company, and that means by me."

Harley didn't want Jade to think he'd come here just to profess his undying love and pick up where they'd left off. He hadn't. He'd gotten over her a long time ago, whether he'd wanted to or not. Going through navy boot camp was enough to push anything other than survival out of his mind. The quiet moments were another matter. Those were harder to get through. That's probably why he'd opted to spend most of his service overseas in the thick of things.

He couldn't help but notice there was a slight flicker of disappointment in her eyes before she smiled and nodded. The attraction seemed to be mutual, even if fleeting. She still seemed conflicted by her attraction to him. "Of course. I appreciate your help with all of this."

There was something in her tone that struck Harley as disingenuous. Did she not want him here, or was it about *why* he was here? He wasn't sure, but since he wasn't going anywhere, he decided to do what he could to quell her concerns. "The hospital hired me, but I want to assure you that I'll be an impartial third party as I investigate what happened. I'm being paid to find the truth, whether that reflects favorably on the hospital or not."

Jade let out a ragged breath and the tension seemed to ease from her shoulders. "I'm relieved to hear you say that. There's no way I could afford to hire my own investigators. And any attorneys I might hire would be more interested in suing the pants off the hospital to get a cut for themselves. I just want to find out the truth."

Harley was surprised. He looked around the house, which was okay, but nothing special. The furniture was worn, and he'd noticed when he pulled up that her car was an older model. Financial security had certainly seemed to be a priority when she'd left him for the more successful Lance, and yet her ex didn't seem to be contributing much to her way of life now. As a young divorcée, wouldn't some kind of settlement from the hospital be important to her? "You're not interested in suing the hospital?"

Jade shrugged. "If they're at fault, I wouldn't turn it down. I can put it toward buying a home or stick it in my retirement account. But what I'm really after..." She hesitated and shook her head. "The truth is that the results of my DNA tests just confirmed what I've always felt deep down inside."

Harley frowned. "And what's that?"

"That I've never belonged." Her dark gaze fixed on him and he felt her raw emotions like a vise squeezing his chest. "I've always felt like a puzzle piece that got tossed into the wrong box. I was never going to fit in and now I know why. So, I want to know where I *do* come from."

"What about Arthur and Carolyn?" Her folks hadn't been particularly fond of Harley—he wasn't the kind of boy any parents wanted dating their teenage daughter—but they'd always seemed like good people. Jade loved them dearly and he'd never suspected that they treated her like anything other than their little princess.

"The parents that raised me will always be my parents, but I want to know who my biological family really is. Where I come from. What my life should've been like, so that something about it can start to make sense."

He didn't know what to say to that. Harley had always thought that Jade had her life together. She was smart and ambitious. She made the most of her every opportunity. The framed certificate on the wall declared that she had her PhD in pharmacology. He'd always thought she was someone who knew who she was and what she wanted. To hear otherwise was unsettling. It made him want to question everything he felt was a fact. It also made him desperately want to uncover the truth for her so she could have some closure.

“Have you always felt so lost, Jade?”

She avoided his gaze for a moment, perhaps knowing instinctively that she couldn’t lie to him. He’d spent many years in the navy learning interrogation techniques. Even if she could’ve lied to him back in high school, she couldn’t now. He’d know the truth.

“Not when I was with you,” she said at last. “That was probably the only time things felt right in my life.”

Harley knew exactly what she meant. He’d spent most of the past decade in a tailspin, trying to right his course after their breakup. He’d lost his True North when Jade left him for Lance, and he really hadn’t recovered. Sure, he’d been successful. He’d moved on with his life. But somehow he knew that there was a hole in his world where Jade belonged. He had yet to find someone or something else to fill it. None of the women he’d dated—and he used that term loosely—fit the bill. Sex was fine, but he never wanted more with any of them.

He’d never dreamed that Jade would feel lost, too.

“I will find out the truth. I intend to find out what happened to you and why. I’ll find your family.”

On reflex, he reached out and took her hand. It felt

small and delicate in his large, rough ones, rousing a protective instinct he wasn't expecting. He'd come here today thinking he would satisfy his curiosity, scratch his itch to work in the field again and perhaps finally be able to move on where Jade was concerned. As she clutched him tightly, he felt the heat of awareness travel up his arm, warming his chest. He remembered this feeling. A feeling that happened only when he touched her.

This was all wrong. His plan had started unraveling the moment she opened the door. This was the exact opposite of what he wanted to happen. He couldn't be attracted to Jade and not end up in the same mess as last time.

Or could he? Maybe he could compartmentalize the attraction and keep it separate from any emotional attachment. It wasn't like they were kids any longer. He'd had plenty of women in his bed without strings, and it had worked fine. If Jade was open to the idea of indulging for old time's sake, it might be exactly what he needed to close the book on the two of them for good. It was a risky proposition—one she might be completely uninterested in—but he had to find a way to get through the next week or two with her constantly on his mind.

"Thank you," she whispered softly.

"I promise you that, and I'm a man of my word." Harley's attention was drawn away from her by a ring tone coming from the kitchen.

"That's my phone. Excuse me one second." Jade got up and left the room, answering the phone after a moment.

Anxious, Harley got up from his seat. He paced around the living room to burn off some of the excess energy running through his veins. Touching her, even just that little bit, had set off a chain reaction in his nervous system. He was suddenly on edge, ready to leap out at the enemy or jump from a plane. There would be no adrenaline payoff in this situation, however. At least not right now or he'd frighten her off. He needed to keep his hands to himself and get through this interview.

He turned and focused on a row of photographs that lined the fireplace mantel. The biggest was a portrait of her and Lance on their wedding day. It made Harley's chest ache to realize how beautiful she'd looked that day. The dress and flowers didn't matter to him; he focused in on her face. She was beaming with excitement, so happy for the future she was going to have with Lance. A future he didn't think she got.

Would things have been different if she had married him instead?

Harley shook away those thoughts because they weren't helpful. In reality, the teenage Harley Dalton would never have been enough for someone like Jade. He had been spinning his wheels, unsure of what he wanted to do with his life. All he knew was that he wanted to spend every waking moment with Jade. That didn't pay very well. His life took the path it had only because of the choice she'd made to be with someone else. He never would've joined the navy, built his own company or made a whole new life for himself if she hadn't walked away from him. If he hadn't felt like he needed to better himself and his situation to be worthy of a woman like her, he might never have worked so hard.

He supposed he should thank her for that, but he wouldn't. Instead, he'd just do his best to crack the case and get her the answers she deserved.

And if he was a smart man, he'd stop there.

"So that's it? He held your hand and asked you a few questions?" Sophie looked across the kitchen table at Jade and wrinkled her nose. "I was expecting more when you said your first love showed up on your doorstep to take on your case."

"That was enough," Jade said with a sigh. "I don't think my heart could've taken much more than that."

Sophie had shown up for their usual Tuesday gathering, eager for all the juicy details. She hadn't lived in Charleston back then, so she didn't know Harley, but she knew Jade had a love that predated Lance. She was eager to dig into that, even if Jade wasn't interested. For the most part, Sophie's life was wrapped up in her work. Being a lawyer took up long hours, leaving her little time for much else. As such, Sophie was always interested in exciting tales to live vicariously. She would also push Jade into situations from time to time. Like doing that news interview after the hospital sent her a letter that politely told her to get bent.

"Was he as cute as you remembered?"

Jade twisted her lips in thought as she pictured the solid wall of man standing in her doorway. "*Cute* isn't the word I'd use for Harley. Cute is for puppies and babies. He was…hot. Ripped-guy-on-the-cover-of-a-romance-novel hot."

Just thinking about him holding her hand was enough to make her face feel warm and her whole body languid. It was an innocent touch. A supportive gesture not meant to titillate or entice, but the impact on Jade had been massive. It had been a long time since a man had touched her. Even longer since a man had looked at her the way Harley had. Her body could recall the feeling instantly, making her want to turn on the fan despite it still being February.

Maybe it was the red wine on an empty stomach. Or a bad mix of alcohol and unfulfilled desires.

"I think you need to sleep with him."

Jade shot to attention in her chair. "What? You're joking, right?"

"Not at all. I think after everything, a hot tryst

with some serious man candy is just what the doctor ordered."

"Harley is not the kind of guy for me to start a relationship with."

"Who said anything about a relationship? I was just thinking about a hot tumble. You don't have to keep him."

Jade could only roll her eyes. It was a tempting thought, but a silly one. Why would someone as successful and handsome as Harley want someone like her? Even short term. He could do better and avoid dealing with the past in the process. "I wouldn't even know what to do with a man like that, to be honest. I'm out of practice and he's not rookie material."

"I need to see a picture of this guy. He doesn't sound like he could be real." Sophie picked up her phone and immediately set off to search for him on the internet. "Nothing is coming up when I hunt for Harley Dalton," she said. "No Facebook. Not even his company website has a photo of him."

"I'm not surprised. With the kind of work he does, I imagine he has a limited online presence. You'll just have to take my word for it."

"For now," Sophie said, making Jade worry that her friend would nose in where she didn't belong. "Next time I come over, I expect you to have hauled out your yearbook, if nothing else."

"What's more important is that the hospital isn't blowing me off now," she said, trying to switch the subject from her hunky ex. "Hiring an investigator is a big step."

Sophie grinned and took a sip of wine. "I told you I knew what I was doing. There's nothing quite like public shame. Now they're going to get to the bottom of the case and you don't have to pay a dime. No reason to worry."

Jade wasn't so sure about that. At this point, she almost wished that her parents had just been lying to her about being adopted. That certainly would've been easier to cope with. Instead, they'd been adamant that she was the baby they'd left the hospital with. She had a tiny birthmark on her hip that her mother had noticed before they went home. What her mom couldn't be sure of was whether or not the baby she'd delivered had had that same birthmark beneath her swaddling blankets and diapers.

"How am I not supposed to worry? This scenario can only end badly. My parents insist I wasn't adopted. The only time and place something could've happened to me was while they were still in the hospital and I was in the nursery. Someone made a huge mistake and two families have paid the price for it."

"That's not an impossible mistake to make. Especially during Hugo."

Jade shook her head and sighed. How had she gotten caught up in something like this? Being switched at birth was the stuff of television movies, but Sophie was right about the storm. It had been a Category Four when it hit Charleston. The whole town was in chaos amid power outages, massive flooding and large numbers of casualties being rushed into the hospitals for treatment.

It sounded like the perfect storm for something to go wrong in, and if something would go wrong, it would happen to Jade. She was a magnet for that sort of thing. But being switched at birth? It was a crazy thought.

The hospital agreed, dismissing the claim as nonsense. And until she'd gone on the news, they would've gladly brushed her off. Instead, they'd hired Dalton Security, a company she now knew was famous for getting the job done no matter what it took. Harley had always been a rule breaker when he felt the cause justified it. Now that seemed to be the company motto. He would do what he was hired to do and find out the truth, although she worried about how many lives would be upended in the process.

Jade set her wineglass on the kitchen table and sat back in her chair. "Maybe this whole thing is a mistake."

"What do you mean?" Sophie asked.

"I mean, maybe I'm digging into something that's better left buried. It's been almost thirty years since the switch happened. I'm looking for answers, but what...what if all I find is heartache? It's going to destroy families."

"Or unite them," Sophie countered. "Your parents

know that you love them, and they love you no matter what they find. That isn't a risk. But I'm willing to bet a part of them would want to know what happened to their biological daughter, too. They have to wonder if she's safe and happy. They wouldn't trade you for the world, but this will bring them peace of mind, if nothing else. You're going to gain family, not lose them."

"You can't be so sure. Maybe my parents will realize their real daughter is so much better than I am, and they'll choose her over me."

"That is the most ridiculous thing I've ever heard. Anyone would be happy to have you for their daughter. I have no idea who you were swapped with, but your parents did not get the short end of the stick with you, Jade."

"I know," she admitted reluctantly. That was her insecurity speaking. Her parents would be shocked to hear her even suggest such a thing. "I just don't like not knowing how any of this will turn out."

Sophie crossed her arms over her chest in exasperation. "Well, you'll never know until you try. And even if you stopped the investigation now, it's too late. The genie is out of the bottle and there's no way you'd be able to pretend you don't know the truth any longer. You might as well follow the trail to see where it leads, or you're always going to wonder and harbor regrets."

Jade frowned at her friend. That's all she could do, because she knew Sophie was right. The minute she got that DNA test in the mail there was no turning back.

"Your biological parents are out there, somewhere. You've always wanted to have that connection to someone that you felt you lacked. You'll have more family now. More people to depend on. More people to love you."

"You make it sound like this is all going to end like a Disney movie. I'm not about to find out I'm a secret princess. Birds aren't going to make my clothes and a prince isn't going to sweep me off my feet. My real parents could be horrible people. And even if they aren't, this is going to end in lawsuits and tears, and maybe even someone going to jail, if we were switched on purpose."

"Maybe. But I'm an optimist. And I think this is going to be good for you. You need some good in your life after everything that happened with Lance."

Jade groaned and pushed herself up from the table. "I don't want to talk about all that tonight."

"We're not. And I didn't mean to bring it up. I'm just saying that I think you deserve some happiness. I think there are good things on the horizon for you. Even if your real family doesn't turn out to be everything you've hoped for, there can still be positives. Maybe you'll get a huge settlement from the hospital and you can buy a nice house. That would be something good."

Jade picked up the half-empty bottle of wine from the counter and carried it back to the table. She refilled both their glasses. "It would certainly help," she admitted. "Lance's addiction ate through all our savings. I'm making decent money now, but things like a house are just pipe dreams with the cost of living in Charleston."

She set the bottle on the table and sat down in the chair. "Things weren't supposed to end up like this, you know? Everyone said that Lance was the smart choice for me. He was older, established, educated… Marrying him was going to provide me with the stable, safe and loving home I wanted for myself and my future family. We wouldn't struggle with money the way my parents did. Everything was supposed to end up perfectly."

"No one could've expected what happened to Lance, honey," Sophie said. "They call it the opioid *epidemic* for a reason. A lot of people get caught up in it without meaning to. He was never the same after that car accident."

"No, he wasn't."

It had been the beginning of the end for their marriage, although Jade didn't know it then. She was too busy fighting her way through her last year of pharmacy school to see the warning signs. He'd needed the pain pills after his back surgery, but the more he took, the harder it was for him to manage things at work. The more stress he was under, the more pills he needed. As he started to fail, Jade had graduated and thrived in her new career as a pharmacist. Lance couldn't cope with the idea of her being more successful than he was, and it just fed into his existing drug problem.

The next thing she knew, the cops were at her door at 2:00 a.m. and she was being questioned about a break-in at the pharmacy where she worked. Apparently, Lance had taken her keys to steal pain pills. His doctors had recognized he had an issue, and refused to give him more pain medication, so he'd resorted to more desperate means to get it. Jade had filed for divorce before Lance could even get a public defender assigned to him. It was one thing to battle addiction, but to put her career at risk in the process seemed like a deliberate move on his part that she couldn't overlook. He couldn't stand her success and she was tired of propping up his ego.

"The irony of it all is that I broke things off with Harley because he was supposedly the bad boy who wouldn't amount to anything. Lance was the good guy with a future. Harley was trouble with an angel's smile that would lead me down the wrong path in life. I can't help but wonder sometimes," Jade said, as she fingered the rim of her wineglass, "what would have happened if I'd made a different choice. Did things work out the way they were meant to?

Or did I go against my gut and make the worst mistake of my life by walking away from him all those years ago?”

And if it had been a mistake, Jade couldn’t help but wonder if Harley showing up on her porch was a second chance to make things right. Did she dare take the risk?

Three

Harley felt like a stupid, insecure teenager again.

That didn't happen very often, and frankly, it was silly that he felt that way now. He was a grown man. A successful CEO of his own company. There was no reason for him to feel anything but completely confident in his skin. But walking up the driveway to the Nolans' house made him just as anxious as it had when he'd picked Jade up for dates all those years ago.

Perhaps because it was the same little house—a brick-and-vinyl rancher with a carport and neglected flower beds. It was an older home in a poorer area of town, but he knew this part of Charleston well. The apartment he'd shared with his mother was only a few blocks away, or it had been, before it was demolished and replaced with a shopping center.

The whole neighborhood seemed quieter now, as though all the children he remembered running the streets were grown and gone. Things seemed to be more in disrepair as owners aged and were unable to maintain their properties or were forced to move out and rent to people who didn't care as much for their begonias as they did.

At one time, Harley had felt like he fitted in around here. Now, with his shiny black Jaguar in the driveway instead of a beat-up old truck, and a designer suit replacing his torn jeans, it was obvious that the neighborhood wasn't the only thing that had changed.

As he faced the front door, where Arthur Nolan had greeted him dozens of times with a sour expression, he was glad he'd asked Jade to meet him here today. He'd already interviewed her, but having her there while he questioned her parents would make things easier.

Or so he thought.

The door opened and he looked up in time to see Jade step into the doorway. She must have come from work because she was wearing black dress pants, heels and a clingy red sweater that was precisely the same shade as her flawlessly applied lipstick. Her blond hair was slicked back into a bun, highlighting her delicate bone structure as she smiled at him. She looked poised, professional and absolutely stunning. He wasn't sure his heart could withstand this version of his high school sweetheart.

"Are you going to come in or just stand out there in the cold?"

"I haven't decided," he replied. "Your dad still got that shotgun?"

Jade looked to her right and nodded. "Right here by the door as always. I doubt he's keen to use it on you any longer. You're safe to come in."

Harley climbed the steps and leaned close to her, drawing in her scent before whispering into her ear. "If he knew the things I did to you back then, he'd shoot me on the spot."

Jade's eyes widened as she took a step back. Her pale skin flushed pink as her lips tightened a bit with amused disapproval. "Best you keep that to yourself," she noted. "Come on in and have a seat. I'll get them both."

Finding himself alone in the living room, he realized not much had changed inside the house, either. The furniture was the same, although the old tube television in the corner had been replaced with a new flat screen. There was also a large framed portrait over the desk of Jade on her wedding day. Unlike the one at her house, this was just her. Her back was turned, showcasing the lace and buttons that traveled down her spine into the intricate train of her dress. She glanced over her shoulder with a coy smile that made him wish she'd been gazing at him that day instead of Lance.

"Look who the cat dragged in," a man's voice boomed from behind him, distracting him from his unhelpful thoughts.

Harley turned around to find a softer, graying version of the Arthur Nolan he remembered. This one didn't glare at him with disapproval, putting Harley slightly more at ease. He smiled and reached out to shake her father's hand. "Good to see you again, sir, although I wish it were under different circumstances."

"Don't I know it," Arthur said with a serious expression. "This has been really hard on Carolyn, and Jade, too. You can't imagine something like this happening to you."

"I'll do everything I can to find the answers for your family."

Arthur nodded and patted him on the upper arm. "Good, good. Let's have a seat. Carolyn is going to be a minute. She's fussing with some coffee."

Harley sat down in a wingback chair that faced the sofa. Arthur sat there, leaving a space for Jade's mother beside him. A moment later, Jade came in with a tray of mugs, cream and sugar. She put it down on the coffee table between them and took a seat in the chair beside Harley. Carolyn followed with a carafe of hot coffee and poured everyone a cup.

"I know it's late in the day, but it's so chilly, I thought we needed something to warm us up."

"Thank you, Mrs. Nolan."

Carolyn looked up at him with a wide smile as she appraised what had become of the boy who had once graced her doorstep. "I think you can call me Carolyn now, dear. You're not a teenage boy sniffing around my daughter any longer."

Harley smiled back and nodded, but there was something in her eyes that made him question her words. There was a curious curl to her lips as she looked him over, then glanced back at her daughter. It made him wonder if perhaps Mrs. Nolan didn't think he was such a bad match for Jade, after all.

Interesting thought, but she was wrong.

"If you don't mind, I'm going to record this interview. It will allow me to focus on the discussion now instead of taking notes, and I can go back and do that later."

Her parents nodded. He started the recorder on his phone and placed it gently on the coffee table between them. "So tell me about the day you checked in to St. Francis to have your daughter."

"It was chaos," Carolyn began. "Everyone was waiting on the storm to hit. Arthur was nailing wood on the windows and sandbagging the sliding door to keep out the water. We'd stockpiled some supplies, and did everything we could do to prepare. And then I went into labor."

She shook her head. "I had another week to go. I thought for sure we'd get through the storm, but no, Jade was ready." She looked at her daughter and a pained expression came across her face. "Well, not Jade. Our biological daughter. It's so hard to come to terms with all of this. I can't think about the baby I raised and not think it was the same Jade in my belly all that time. Who would do such a thing?"

Harley noticed tears glittering in Carolyn's eyes. Tears weren't his specialty, but he could cope. He'd learned he was better at keeping interviewees focused than he was at consoling them. "I understand this is hard for you," he said. "Just go over what you remember about your time at the hospital."

Arthur put his hand over Carolyn's and squeezed it. "We made it to the hospital before the storm hit," he continued. "We had a few hours to go and were worried about a long labor, since it was our first baby, but our daughter arrived rather quickly and without a fuss if you don't count me fainting. It's hard to believe, but having a baby was the easiest thing about that day. About two hours later, the power went out. The wind picked up. All hell broke loose. Since the nursery didn't have any windows, they recommended that the babies stay there for their own safety. It broke Carolyn's heart because she'd barely gotten a chance to hold the baby before she was taken away. Maybe if we'd spent more time with her…"

Harley hated to hear the Nolans blame themselves. He didn't know what had happened, but he knew it wasn't anything they did wrong. "Don't beat yourself up about this. From what I understand, newborns all look very similar, especially in those first few hours. It takes time for their individual features and personalities to come out. You went through a lot that day and had no reason to question the staff."

Arthur nodded, but Harley could tell he still blamed himself somehow. "After the storm went through, things weren't much better. There was only emergency power. Most of the staff was downstairs in the ER. There were only maybe two or three nurses working the whole maternity ward and I'd say there were easily nine or ten mothers there at the time."

"Did any of the staff or people you saw at the hospital seem off to you? Anything at all strike you as odd?"

Carolyn furrowed her brow in thought. "Nothing other than the hurricane. The staff were stressed out but they seemed really focused on keeping everything afloat. There was even one nurse, I forget her name, who sat and chatted with me for a while. She was so sweet. I can't believe I can't remember her name now. But everyone was great. Did you notice anything, Arthur?"

He shook his head. "Everyone seemed to be coping. That's all anyone could do. If anything seemed strange, I chalked it up to that."

"How long was it until you got to really spend time with Jade?"

"The next day," Carolyn said. "By then the power was back on and things seemed to be closer to normal. I got to spend most of the day with her. That's when I first noticed that birthmark on her leg. That means the switch had already taken place, doesn't it?"

It did. Harley knew exactly which birthmark she was referring to, although he wouldn't say as much to her parents. It was crescent shaped and high on Jade's upper thigh. He'd kissed it a dozen times in his youth. "It sounds like it."

Carolyn started crying in earnest and Arthur comforted her. The conversation continued on for another half hour or so, but Harley had already gotten what he needed. The switch had happened early, during the storm itself. That at least narrowed the window in terms of hospital staff and visitors with access to the babies.

Harley knew he should be focused on the parents as they continued, but he had a hard time not watching Jade's expression as they spoke about that day. About the birth of the child that wasn't her. Speaking about the arrival of the baby they adored, but didn't come home with. It was hard for her to hear, he could tell. It was hard for them, too, but it was her pained face that drew his gaze.

He hated seeing her like this. Harley was no knight in shining armor come to save Jade; he knew that much. But perhaps he could set this situation to rights for her. He'd done his research on her since their interview and had found himself at a loss as he stared at his computer screen. She had been sold false goods with Lance and now she was paying for it. Finding out her ex was serving time was surprising to Harley, so he knew it had to have blindsided Jade. She'd put all her faith in him, and Lance had destroyed their future together.

Harley supposed that another man in his shoes might think it was her karmic retribution for spurning him all those years ago. But he had loved Jade too much to ever wish ill on her back then. He'd just wanted her to be happy. And now, he wanted to help. Not by sweeping her off her feet, as much as the idea of carrying her off to bed appealed to him.

No, all he could do was find the truth for Jade and hope that she could be happy at last, knowing where she really belonged.

* * *

Jade walked Harley to his car when the interview was over. It was dark now, with the winter evenings still coming early. She was looking forward to spring, with warmer temperatures and maybe the chance to work in the garden. To get to that, though, she first had to make it through this investigation with Harley.

"I hope my parents were helpful," she said, as they reached his car.

"They were. As helpful as they could be considering they weren't involved. If nothing else, I was able to narrow the timeline down. You were switched almost immediately after you were born. Probably during the worst of the storm, when everything was at its most frantic. It was a crime of opportunity, in my opinion."

"A crime? As in someone actually did it on purpose?" Jade had lain in bed for several nights wondering how any of this could've happened, but she'd rarely considered it might be deliberate. "I could see if it was a mistake in the chaos, but you really think someone did it on purpose?"

"I do." Harley crossed his muscled forearms over his chest and leaned back against his shiny sports car. It was so sleek and low to the ground she wondered how he even got in and out of the thing.

"To what end? What did it get them? I can't see how anyone would benefit from it."

"That I don't know yet. I'll find out one way or another. But in my gut, I know it was done intentionally. They may not have known in advance which babies and when, but they saw their chance during the storm and took it."

They. He kept saying that with an intense expression on his face that both frightened and thrilled her. Who was he talking about? Jade had a hard time imagining what kind of person would do something like that. Then again, people were surprising her a lot lately. That reminded her… She reached into her pocket and pulled out a note she'd received the day before.

"Harley, before you go, I want you to take a look at this. It came in the mail yesterday. I thought it might factor into your investigation."

Harley took the letter from her and unfolded it carefully. His gaze went over the text again and again, with his expression darkening more each time. His jaw was clenched tight in anger when he finally looked up at her.

"Why didn't you mention this sooner?"

Jade stiffened as his wave of rage was aimed in her direction. She wasn't expecting that. Was he really upset with her? She took a step back on reflex. "I wanted you to speak with my parents first. They don't know about the letter and I don't want them to know."

Her parents were dealing with enough right now

without knowing that Jade had received a threatening letter from some anonymous whack job. And to be honest, she wasn't too concerned. She'd just appeared on television. Any weirdo sitting at home watching the news could've written her that letter.

"Do you have any idea who would've sent this to you?"

Jade shook her head. The handwritten text was fairly straightforward—let it go or else. That could be from anyone. "I thought maybe someone from the hospital wanted me to back off. They were basically shamed into cooperating when I went public with my story. I'm sure there's someone there who wishes I would just go away. Or someone that saw me on TV. I wasn't taking it too seriously."

Harley narrowed his gaze at her. "You need to take it seriously, Jade. If nothing else, because whoever sent this knows your home address. That's a problem. Are you listed in the phone book or online?"

Jade's spine straightened at that thought. She'd been so preoccupied with other things that she hadn't thought about that aspect of it. A chill ran through her and she snuggled farther into her favorite sweater. She wished she'd brought a coat out here with her, but she hadn't anticipated a long conversation. "No. It's a rental so you'd think there wouldn't be anything associating my name with the house, but I suppose you can find anything on the internet for a price."

That made the corners of Harley's full mouth turn down into a frown. It made her want to reach out and rub her thumb across his bottom lip the way she had before. The dark, angry storm in his eyes, however, kept her arms firmly crossed over her chest where they belonged.

"Do you have the envelope it came in?" he asked.

She nodded and pulled it out of her pocket. "Here. What are you going to do with it?"

Harley reached into the breast pocket of his coat and pulled out a plastic specimen bag. He put both the letter and the envelope inside and sealed it up. "I'm going to send it to my lab along with the DNA swabs I took of you and your parents. I'll see if they can pull some prints or DNA off of it. I might need to get prints from you later so we can exclude yours."

"You have your own lab?" *And you keep evidence bags in your coat?* She kept the last part to herself. She got the feeling he wouldn't understand why she thought it was weird.

Harley nodded. "It's a necessity. Local police investigations are stymied by the backlog awaiting lab testing. Since I have my own state-of-the-art lab in DC, none of my investigators have to wait. Things can move forward faster. It was one of the first things I invested in when the company started to gain success."

Jade tried not to look impressed, but it was hard. The Harley she was looking at was so different from the one she remembered. At least on the outside. On the inside, she was pretty sure the rebel was still there. He might have a sports car instead of his old truck, but he probably still drove fast. And no doubt liked to bend the rules as far as he could. That had always made her nervous back when they were dating, and still did now. She could look at Harley but not touch. And definitely not keep.

"Anyway, the results might help us narrow down who might be involved. Maybe the person who was behind the switch sent the letter. Or someone else who knows something about the case." He put it away and looked at her with a softer expression on his face. "Is this the first note you've received?"

"Yes."

"Anything else unusual? Phone calls? The feeling that someone is following you?"

Jade sighed and tried to think back over the last week since she'd gone on the news and her story had spread across Charleston. It had been chaotic to be sure, but she hadn't felt like she was in danger. "Nothing I can think of. I lead a pretty quiet, boring life compared to yours, Harley."

"Good," he said with a curt nod. "That was what you wanted, after all, right? Safe, comfortable? All the things you didn't think I could give you."

She had been waiting for this moment. He'd been so professional thus far, but she knew eventually he would mention their breakup. How could he not?

"I don't know what you could've given me. We were kids and I made the best decision I could at the time. I ended up being all wrong about Lance, but I could've been wrong about you, too. But something tells me you weren't interested in a quiet life back then and you're not interested in it now."

He shrugged, confirming in her mind that it was true. "A little excitement isn't all bad, Jade." He pushed off his car to come closer to her, suddenly invading her personal space.

One moment she thought he was irritated with her over their breakup, and the next she could feel his body heat as he moved nearer. Jade looked up at his dark blue eyes, which were virtually black in the dwindling evening light. When he looked at her like that, she could feel her belly clench and her neck and shoulders tense. He could bring some excitement into her life for sure. She had sorely missed that kind of thrill. Unfortunately, with Harley there was always the promise of more than she bargained for.

"I'll, uh, take your word for it," she said. Jade forced herself to take a step back, when every nerve in her body urged her to take a step forward into his arms. The way he looked at her was practically a dare. It was a dare she wanted to take on, but that was exactly why she moved away.

The last thing she needed was her father out on the porch again with his shotgun.

Harley sighed, but she could tell he wasn't going to push the issue. Not here. Not now. But eventually she wouldn't be able to run.

"Well, listen, you're probably freezing, so I'm going to go. I plan to stop by where I'm staying for a few things and then I'll meet you back at your house."

Jade hesitated, wondering what she'd just missed in the conversation while she'd wrestled with her desires. Had she gotten lost in his big blue eyes and not heard him say he was coming to her home? "What? Why are you coming by?"

He patted his suit coat pocket and the letter he'd put inside. "Someone is threatening you, Jade. This is serious. You need someone to protect you."

"You?" He was joking with her, right?

"Of course, me. I don't have any other staff in Charleston right now. Is that a problem?" He arched his brow at her, upping the ante of the dare.

Yes, it was a problem. In a dozen different ways, yes, but she voiced the least complicated one she could come up with. "There's no way I could afford to pay you for security detail, Harley. I don't have any savings left after what happened with Lance."

His brows knitted together in a heavy frown. "You should know better than that, Jade. I'm not doing this for the money."

"But I—"

He reached up and pressed a finger to her lips to silence her argument. "Consider it pro bono work. I need all the tax deductions I can get."

She took another step back in retreat from his touch despite her desire to move closer and let him press his lips to her mouth instead of his fingertip. "Don't I get any say in this? I don't recall asking you to—"

"Nope," he interrupted. "If I know you, and I'm pretty sure I do, you're not going to take this situation seriously. I'm here to do that for you." He smiled and walked away from her. He opened the driver's side door to his car and hesitated. "I'll be there in about an hour."

Jade watched him back out of the driveway and disappear down her parents' street. Her stomach was aching with worry even as her blood still hummed hot in her veins.

Being close to Harley was dangerous. And now she was going to be around him more than she'd ever anticipated. What was she going to do? It was one thing to see him in short visits, but if he was staying with her? Sleeping feet away in her guest bedroom? Would she be able to resist the pull he had on her?

Jade prayed this investigation would be finished quickly. Her reignited libido couldn't take this for too long.

Four

"So, let me get this straight," Harley began, with an exasperated expression on his face. "You're a single woman living alone with no alarm system or means to protect yourself if something happened."

Jade had only expected Harley to show up and get settled in for the night. It was late enough when he arrived. She didn't expect him to do a full home investigation, but then again, this was what he did for a living. So far, nothing nefarious could be found, but now that he was finished, it was time for the inevitable lecture about her personal security.

Jade wasn't really listening. She was too distracted by watching him work, her gaze drawn to his clenched jaw and brow furrowed with concern.

He took it all very seriously. He was very thorough, she had to admit. He'd studied her windows more closely than she ever had. She'd never even opened them before, so she couldn't tell him if they had locks or not.

"This neighborhood is pretty quiet," she argued when he looked at her with dismay. "I'm not aware of any criminal activity that would send me running after an alarm system."

She had initially been worried about having Harley's hulking presence in her house. Every room felt smaller with him in it and she had no escape from him. He was a constant reminder of her past, of her current predicament and of what she couldn't have in the future. That seemed less important now as he was nitpicking every aspect of her home.

Jade liked this little house. It was the first place she'd ever had by herself. She'd moved from her college dorm to Lance's house, then they bought another house together when they moved to Virginia Beach with his work. This was all hers. Her life was all hers. She didn't have a husband to tell her what to do any longer and she didn't need Harley to take over the role.

Harley just shook his head. "It's all got to change, Jade. If you're not comfortable with guns, that's fine, but you've got to have something in place to keep you safe. Maybe a stun gun. The noise alone is usually enough to deter an attacker."

"An attacker?" How had they gone from a threatening letter to break-ins and physical assaults? "It was one letter. And you're here now. That's all I need, right?"

"Yes, I'm here, but I won't be around all the time. You need more protection here than you've got." He whipped his smartphone from his hip and started typing with a flurry of thumbs. "That's about to change."

"What are you doing?"

"I'm emailing Isaiah with my East Coast surveillance team. I'm going to have him send down someone to secure the home and make it safe for you to be here alone."

Jade's eyes grew large. That sounded intense. And expensive. "Harley, I—"

"It's not going to cost you anything," he interrupted, holding up his palm. Apparently, he'd come to anticipate her concerns before she voiced them.

"How is that possible?" It cost someone something. Jade might not be rich, but she wasn't in a position to happily accept handouts, either. Especially from Harley.

He glared at her. "Please don't argue with me about this. It will make me feel better. This is what I do for a living, remember? Whoever wrote you that note wants to scare you into dropping your search for answers. If you're going to continue, and I think you should, you need to be smart about it."

She sighed and shook her head. It was too late to waste any more energy on this. If he wanted to put armed guards in her trees to leap down on intruders, she'd let him. It had been a long day and she was ready for bed.

While she'd been fairly nonchalant about receiving that note when she'd spoken to Harley, it was only because she'd stayed up most of the previous night convincing herself it was nothing. She'd never expected anything like this to happen, and when it had, she'd been taken aback. By the time she'd fallen asleep, it was almost time to get up. She usually opened at the pharmacy, which allowed her to get off in early afternoon, but that didn't make it any less painful when her alarm went off at five.

Jade looked over at Harley, who was still typing furiously into his phone. Part of his business was in alarms and surveillance, so she shouldn't be surprised he'd want that done here. Maybe that would make him feel comfortable enough that he wouldn't have to sleep here every night. She hoped so.

And yet she didn't.

It was confusing being around Harley again. More confusing than she'd expected it to be. She thought she'd gotten over him a long time ago, but whenever he got close to her, her body responded as though it remembered him. She felt this desperate urge to reach out and touch him. For him to touch her. It was a ridiculous and inappropriate thought about the man who'd been hired to investigate her case. She knew that. Apparently she had made a mistake going too long without male companionship after her divorce. Harley had showed up unexpectedly and here she was, ripe for the picking.

As much as the idea of being plucked by Harley was appealing to her neglected body, her head knew better. He was not the one for her. She'd overridden her body before, and she knew she could do it again. The only difference this time was that Harley was so close, and would be for who knew how long. It was easier before, when she could just break off with him and return to college, where she didn't have to see him every day.

But she could stay strong. She had to. It wasn't smart to muddy the investigation with personal feelings. And feelings where Harley was concerned were a terrible idea. He might be attracted to her, but there were times when she got the sense he didn't want to be. If they did hook up, that would be all there was to it. Neither one of them seemed keen to make the same mistake again.

"Okay, that's done," he announced, then slipped the phone back into its holster on his belt. "They'll probably be out the day after tomorrow or so to get you set up."

Jade just nodded. It wasn't a bad idea, really. It would give her some peace of mind. "Thanks. It's getting late, so if you've got all your things, I'll let you get settled in for the night," she said. The sooner she got him settled in for the night, the sooner she could put a couple walls between the two of them.

"Great." Harley bent to pick up the small overnight bag and larger garment bag he'd brought into the house with him.

She led him down the hallway toward the bedrooms. The little bungalow had been perfect when she was looking for a place. Since it was just her, two bedrooms and a single bath were all she needed. Now, as she stood in the hallway and realized the two beds were technically only about eight feet apart, she wished her place was a little larger.

"This is the guest room." She opened the door to the small room that had yet to house any actual guests. She used it mostly for an office and storage, but she'd put a sofa sleeper in there just in case someone needed to stay. "I went ahead and unfolded the sofa bed. It has clean sheets and blankets on it, but if you get cold, there's another in the closet. You probably saw it earlier, but the bath is here at the end of the hallway. There's just the one to share."

Harley eyed the space and then turned back to her. "And you're right across the hall?"

She gestured to the closed door. "Yes. That's me."

"Okay, great." He threw his bags down on the bed and switched on the little bedside lamp.

She watched him circle the small space like a Great Dane trying to get comfortable in a tiny bed made for a Chihuahua. Finally, he sat on the edge of the bed and the metal frame and springs gave a loud squeak of protest. She closed her eyes in embarrassment and wished she'd bought a regular bed for here. It would've taken up most of the room, but would have been better for company. Especially tall, muscular company.

It occurred to her that he would be more comfortable at his nice hotel suite or wherever he was staying. Heck, he'd probably be more comfortable in a sleeping bag on the front porch. He shouldn't suffer because he felt the need to protect her. "You don't have to do this," she said.

He looked at her, his blue eyes searching her face for a moment, and then he smiled in a way that made her stomach clench. "I know I don't. Good night, Jade."

His words were a gentle dismissal to keep her from trying to talk him out of this. He was obviously too stubborn and would stay here no matter what. Jade had to appreciate his dedication, if nothing else. "Good night, Harley."

She left his room, pulling the door closed behind her and crossing the narrow hallway to her own room. Shutting the second door, she leaned back against the wood and felt her body finally starting to relax. She hadn't realized it until she was alone again, but she was strung tight as a drum when she was around Harley. It was emotionally and physically exhausting to be so close to him after all this time. The attraction between them, long-suppressed and bubbling just below the surface, was at constant odds with her sense of self-preservation. Keeping everything in check was a balancing act she wasn't sure she could keep up much longer.

Dropping onto her own bed, she stared at the door. She supposed she should be happy to feel something. After everything that had happened with Lance, she'd almost become numb. Her mother actually thought there was something wrong with her because she hadn't cried over the divorce. It was as though she was in a state of shock that didn't allow her to feel anything at all.

She'd stayed there, stuck in limbo all this time, snapping out of it only when she'd received that DNA test.

Then, suddenly, all her emotions were flipped back on like a switch and her whole body was a bundle of raw nerves. She spent all day on the verge of tears or laughter, never quite sure which one was ready to burst from her without provocation. Could she risk unleashing that kind of pent-up energy on Harley?

With a sigh, she slipped out of her heels and got ready for bed. Maybe she would be exhausted enough to fall into a deep sleep and forget that Harley was only feet away.

Somehow, she doubted it.

* * *

A loud crash snapped Harley out of a restless sleep as his tailbone whacked the ground. It was only then that he realized the springs had given way on the sofa bed and he was lying on the hard wooden floor with only the thin mattress beneath him.

A pounding of fists at the door came next. "Harley, are you okay?"

"Yes, I'm fine. The bed is another matter."

The door slowly opened and Jade stuck her head inside as she switched on the overhead light. Her face was washed clean of makeup and her long, pale hair was loose around her shoulders. For a minute, as he looked at her, it was as though she were seventeen again. Beautiful. Natural. Just the way he remembered her when he thought back on their time together.

Until she started laughing at him.

She held it in at first, but he could see the facade start to crumble as her hand went to cover her mouth. The giggles escaped from her lips, making him glance down at himself. He really did look ridiculous sprawled across the lopsided mattress, in a tangle of blankets. He had to laugh, too. He was too damn big for a bed like this and he should've known better than to even try sleeping on it. He'd tried not to move too much once he got into bed, but once he was asleep, he couldn't help it. He'd rolled over and—*BOOM.*

They both laughed for a moment, their ever-looming tension finally dissipating with the emotional release. He supposed it was worth making an ass of himself if it helped break the ice between them. It would be a long and awkward assignment if they never got past it.

He shook his head and started checking out the sofa bed. He thought perhaps he could put it back together, but the hooks of the metal springs had actually ripped through the plastic fabric that held up the mattress. This thing wasn't fixable. He would buy her a new sofa bed. A sturdier one. Maybe just an actual bed, with box springs and a steel frame.

Harley threw back the blankets with a heavy sigh and Jade's laughter abruptly silenced. He looked down at himself again and realized he wasn't wearing anything but a snug pair of black Calvin Klein boxer briefs. He wasn't much for pajamas, but hadn't thought about it until he exposed himself. When he glanced back at Jade, he realized her eyes were fixed on his chest and stomach, her mouth agape. It was probably a different sight than she remembered. His whole body had changed over the years. He'd been a scrawny kid back then. Now he was a solid man made of muscle and covered in coarse, dark brown hair.

When she finally closed her mouth, a curious smirk formed at the corners of her lips. Jade seemed to like what she saw. And he liked that she liked it. He just wasn't sure what he should do about that glassy look in her eyes. Probably nothing. Maybe everything.

He got up from the shambles of the bed, wrapped the blanket around himself and snatched his pillow from the floor. His movements seemed to jerk Jade from her intense study and make her realize what she was doing. When her eyes met his again, he couldn't help smiling with amusement. Her cheeks flushed red as she seemed to realize that he'd caught her staring at him. With any other woman, he would've walked up to her, dropped the blanket and let her look and touch her fill. He wasn't shy, especially when he wanted something. Or someone.

But not with Jade. Things were too damn complicated between them for that. If there was one lesson he'd learned in the military, it was that life went the smoothest when he was in control. His existence before that point had been a mess as he spiraled through situations he didn't have a handle on. After his service ended, he'd applied that principle to every part of his life and things were infinitely better. He had the distinct feeling that maintaining control would be more difficult with Jade in the picture.

"This bed is toast. I guess I'll just move to the couch in the living room," he said. It might not be more comfortable, but it wouldn't collapse on him. Hopefully.

"Don't be silly," Jade said with a shake of her head. "The living room furniture is okay for sitting, but it's awful for sleeping. I couldn't afford anything nicer. But I have a king-size bed in my room. There's plenty of room for you there."

Harley arched a brow at her. She wanted to share her bed? After the way she'd looked at him just now, he wasn't sure that was such a good idea. She might not admit it to him, or even to herself, but she wanted to touch him and reacquaint herself with his body. And he wanted to let her. "I don't know about that, Jade."

She stuck out her chin defiantly. "We're adults, Harley. Surely we can sleep in the same bed without an issue. If it makes you feel better, I promise to keep my hands to myself." She held up three fingers in the Girl Scout salute before opening the door the rest of the way.

Harley now got a good look at the little cotton nightgown she was wearing to bed. It was short, with the lacy trim skimming her upper thighs. The fabric was pale pink, and transparent enough for him to see the rosy shade of her nipples as they pressed against it. The light from her bedroom behind her highlighted her figure through it, showcasing her narrow waist and the slight curve of her hips.

He swallowed hard. "I promise nothing," he said in a gruff voice. He didn't like to go back on his word, so he didn't make promises he knew he couldn't keep. As it was, he was clutching his pillow in front of himself to hide his pulsating desire. How could such a sweet, innocent piece of clothing stir such a reaction in him?

Probably because Jade could wear a clown suit and he would still want her. That was the long and short of the matter. He might not like it. He might even try to convince himself that he didn't harbor such a strong attraction to Jade any longer. But it was a damned lie. She'd hurt him when she chose Lance, even if he didn't want to admit that to himself. And he could tell himself he didn't need someone in his life who didn't think he was good enough for them. But somehow all that flew out the window where she was concerned.

"Come on," she said with a laugh, and left the doorway, seemingly oblivious to the heated thoughts running through his mind.

Did she think he was being funny? He wasn't sure, but he was running out of sleeping options if he was going to stay here and keep her safe. Once the security equipment was up, he could return to his bed at his mother's house, but until then, he needed someplace to get some decent rest. Reluctantly, Harley followed her out of the guest room and glared across the hallway to Jade's bedroom. He could see the large bed with the floral quilt tossed back and half a dozen decorative pillows piled on the unoccupied side.

While he stood there, Jade leaned across the mattress to snatch the extra pillows off the bed. As she stretched for the last one, the hem of her nightie crept higher and higher, until he could see the firm cheeks of her bottom peeking out from baby blue cotton panties. Not a thong or cheeky cutouts. They were sweet. Innocent. Just like the kind he'd fantasized about peeling off of her back in high school.

He curled his hands into fists. The universe was testing him; that's what it was. There was no other explanation.

"Here you go." Jade pulled back the comforter and patted the mattress in an invitation his eighteen-year-old self would've killed to get.

Harley swallowed hard and made his way around the bed to his side. She was right. It was a big bed, and there was plenty of space. He just knew there wasn't a bed big enough for it not to be a temptation with her so close by.

"Thank you," he said, as he slipped under the blankets. Her sheets were butter-soft and smelled like lavender, just as she always did. It was almost enough to lure him into a state of comfort that would allow him to forget where he was and who was beside him.

Almost.

As it was, he lay on his back, every inch of him stiff as a board. He didn't want to relax enough that he might brush against her under the sheets. He closed his eyes and tried to will himself to sleep.

Moments later, in the dark stillness of her bedroom, he heard Jade's soft voice from beside him. "You know, I never thought I'd share a bed with you, Harley."

His eyes fluttered open, but he kept them pinned on her ceiling fan as he chuckled. "No, me, neither. If I'd kept you out past eleven your father would've had me arrested. Keeping you overnight… I'd be dead."

Jade laughed, too, the melodic sound bringing back memories of them in the back of his pickup truck, looking at the stars. He remembered lying there, gazing into those big doe eyes and feeling his heart slipping away to the smartest girl in school.

Against his better judgment he rolled onto his side now and looked at her. Even in the darkness he could see her facing him, her white-blond hair sprawled across her pillowcase. Her head was resting on her hands as she watched him with curiosity in her eyes. He longed to reach out and cup her cheek and let his thumb drag gently across her bottom lip. Instead, he balled his fists beneath his pillow.

"It was a mistake, you know."

Harley frowned at her. "What was?"

"Choosing Lance."

"I read about what happened with him, and his drug problem. I'm sorry about all that."

"That's not what I meant. I mean that I hurt you, and I never wanted to do that."

Harley wasn't expecting an apology and he wasn't sure how to accept it. "It was for the best." He said the words, but didn't believe them.

"Maybe so. Perhaps things happen the way they're intended to. But lying here next to you after all this time makes me wish I'd gotten one last kiss before I let you go. I probably regret that more than anything else."

Without thinking, Harley surged forward and pressed his lips to hers. He'd had those regrets, too, and now, having her so near, he couldn't fight it anymore. He had to touch her, taste her, even if it was just to convince himself that his memories of her were wrong. She couldn't possibly be everything he'd built her up to be in his mind. She'd become a fantasy because he couldn't have her. The reality would no doubt disappoint him. He hoped that once the kiss was done he could put aside his attraction to her and focus on the case.

He couldn't have been more wrong. Jade melted into his arms, moaning softly against his mouth. She wrapped her body around him, pulling him close to her. He could feel every inch of her curves as they pressed against him beneath the thin cotton of that nightgown. As one of his hands held her face to his, the other drifted down her side, stopping just as it reached the lacy edge of her pajamas. If he crossed that line, he knew there was no going back.

She was everything he remembered and more, his impulsive experiment backfiring in spectacular fashion. It took all he had to realize it and pull away.

The moment their lips parted, Harley felt reality start to close in on him. What the hell was he doing? He was here to protect Jade and find out what had happened at the hospital. Not to manhandle her and start something up between them that he might regret. Yes, it was just a kiss, but he could feel his grip on his self-control slipping away. The way she responded, the soft noises she made… He had to put some distance between them or things were going to go too far. He rolled away, grabbed his pillow and climbed out of bed.

"Where are you going?" Jade asked breathlessly.

"To the couch."

Her face wrinkled with displeasure as she looked up at him from the bed. Everything about her beckoned him to come back. To cross the line. "It was just a kiss. You don't have to go."

Harley had been waiting for an invitation and this was it. If he could accept it. Instead, he shook his head and walked around the foot of the bed to the door. "Yes, I do."

Without looking back at her, he marched down the hallway to the living room. He wrapped himself in the blanket and curled up on the couch so he would fit. With a sigh, he closed his eyes and wished for sleep.

The universe was definitely testing him. And it could kiss his ass.

Five

That kiss was a recipe for insomnia.

Jade was a fool for letting it happen, a fool for wanting it. But she did. If she hadn't, she wouldn't have started that ridiculous conversation. She would've closed her eyes and gone to sleep, keeping her hands to herself the way she'd promised. No, instead she'd pushed him until he broke, and it was everything she'd imagined a kiss with him could be. The reward was short-lived, though, as moments later she was alone in bed with a pounding heart and a liquid center.

Once Harley left for the couch, Jade had lain there staring up at the ceiling fan and trying to figure out what the hell she was doing. She was the one who'd broken it off back then. Teasing Harley with the goods she'd once deprived him of was cruel to them both. They had no business kissing, much less doing anything else. They'd both moved on from their high school days. A physical relationship between them would be nothing more than a complication she couldn't afford, with him around 24/7 trying to protect her.

But at that moment, none of that had mattered. All she'd wanted was a kiss. A touch. To feel desired again after years of thinking she wasn't enough for a man. Lance had stopped touching her after his car accident. It had been pretty serious, resulting in back surgery that would never really fix the problem or get rid of the pain. Months later, when she'd hoped perhaps they could get back to the way things were, he'd decided the rush of popping a roxy was better. He hadn't told her that, though. He'd said he hurt, or just plain avoided the subject. He'd stayed up late, knowing she went to bed early. He'd pulled away whenever she came too close.

It might've been a stupid thing to do, but last night had felt damn good. It had made her feel like a desirable woman for the first time in a long while.

This morning, she was a *sleepy* desirable woman.

Normally she went straight to the shower, but she needed some caffeine first. Jade pulled on her chenille robe and nearly crawled from the bed to the living room, where she found Harley on the couch, already awake. He actually looked as though he was well into his day. He was fully dressed, in a pair of pressed khaki pants and a dark blue shirt, and surrounded by paperwork he was reading through. There was an empty coffee mug in front of him on the table and his blanket was folded neatly over the back of the couch. Apparently he hadn't slept much, either.

"Good morning," she said, as she moved past him into the kitchen.

"Good morning."

Jade poured herself a cup of coffee. When she turned around, Harley was standing in the doorway of the kitchen. She eyed the fully dressed man who dominated the room with his presence. "Did you not sleep at all? That couch is miserable, I told you."

"I slept enough for me. I'm usually awake by four, anyway. If I can get four or five hours a night, I'm good. I've survived on less."

Jade shook her head. "I'm jealous. If I don't get eight, I'm a zombie."

"You didn't get eight last night," he noted. "That's my fault."

"It's the sofa bed's fault." She took a sip of her coffee and tilted her head back. "You'll notice these dark circles under my eyes. That's a sure sign of my undead state."

He studied her face for a moment and shook his head. "I don't see anything. You look beautiful, as always."

"You must still be half-asleep," Jade argued. "I just stumbled out of bed, I've got crazy hair and I'm wearing a bathrobe. Nothing about that is beautiful."

"Nope. I've gone on a four-mile run, taken a shower, had coffee, read through some paperwork and cleaned my gun. I'm very much awake. You're just stubborn."

"Stubborn?" She set down her coffee in surprise.

"Yes. I'm not sure what happened between you and Lance. I only know how it ended. But what I do know is that he didn't take the opportunity he had. If he had appreciated the gift you'd given him by being in his life, he would've cherished it. He would've told you how beautiful and smart and amazing you are. Then you would believe someone when they gave you a compliment instead of arguing with them about it. It's a shame, really."

Jade was stunned by his words. She hadn't really thought about it that way, but he was onto something. She shouldn't let Lance's influence take over her new life, too. "You're right. Let's start over. Tell me I'm beautiful again."

Harley smiled. "Now you're just fishing for compliments, but okay. You look beautiful this morning."

Jade did her best to return his smile with a genuine one of her own. "Thank you."

"See? That wasn't so hard, was it?"

"Me accepting a compliment is like you following the rules. We can do it when we're put on the spot, but it's not instinctual."

"I can follow rules," he said, with a frown lining his forehead.

That made Jade laugh out loud. "Sure you can. That's why you were always in detention."

"That was before the navy. In the military, you follow the rules or you get punished. You obey the chain of command or someone gets hurt."

"So you're saying your bad boy days are behind you?" Jade asked curiously.

A wicked grin spread across his face, one that made Jade want to melt into his arms. He leaned in and pinned her with his baby blues. "Once a bad boy, always a bad boy, Jade. That doesn't change. These days I'm just better at knowing when the punishment is worth the payoff. It usually is."

Her eyes widened as he grew closer, his gaze drifting to her lips. It was enough to make her clutch her coffee mug for dear life. If she had her hands free, who knew what she might do. Reach for him? Touch him? Bad boys certainly had their appeal. She wished they didn't. Things would be easier in her life.

"Today, I work until four," she said, abruptly changing the subject. She turned away from him, fished into the junk drawer and pulled out a spare key to the house. "I'm not sure what's on your agenda, but since you refuse to go to your hotel and sleep in a comfortable bed with room service, here's a key."

Harley reached out and plucked the object dangling from her hand. Jade noticed he did it without touching her, even after leaning in to tease her the moment before. It made her wonder if it was deliberate on his part. Touching each other seemed to lead down a path neither of them were eager to travel.

"Just so you know, I'm not staying at a hotel. I've been staying with Mom while I'm in town. It's a bit out of the way, though, so your place is more convenient. Thanks for the key. I'll be out and about today, but I will make a point of being back by the time you get home."

Jade planted her hands on her hips. He made it seem like a bogeyman was going to leap out of a cabinet at any moment. He didn't appear to be the kind to overreact, but one little letter had really set him on edge. "You don't have to. You're being paid to research the case, not babysit me."

Harley slipped the key into his pocket and sighed. "I know what I'm being paid for. And I can have it done by four."

"Okay," Jade said. She wasn't about to argue with him. It would give her some peace of mind that he was here, she had to admit. "Anything exciting on your agenda today?"

"I think I'm going to the hospital to meet with

them and go over their data. They've pulled a lot of the records from the archives for me to search through. They weren't digitized back then, unfortunately, so that means a lot of shuffling through old papers in someone's abandoned cubicle."

"Sounds like a long, boring day ahead." She held up the coffee carafe, swirling around the last inch of black brew in the bottom. "You can finish this off."

Harley just shrugged, holding out his mug for her to refill it. "It can't all be tracking bad guys and apprehending suspects. Sometimes the paperwork is the most important part. That's where the truth usually lies."

"People don't tell the truth?" she asked.

"They tell the truth as best they know it. Or as they believe it to be."

That was a cynical way of looking at things. "And what about your plans for tomorrow?"

"What's tomorrow?"

"It's my day off. That, and Sundays. Are you going to sit around and look at me all day? Or work your case?"

Harley's lips twisted into a frown. "I'll have to figure that out. I wasn't expecting you to be off during the week, but it's my fault for not asking."

"I could help you with your research," Jade suggested. She was anxious to have answers and she didn't mind doing some of the legwork.

He stiffened and shook his head briskly. "No,

sorry. I can't have you around while I'm investigating. You're too close to the case. It wouldn't be right."

"Oh, so now you follow the rules. You won't break them when it benefits me? I guess it isn't worth the payoff in this scenario."

That earned her a sigh and a roll of his eyes. "I don't want any of my findings called into question, okay? I'll figure out what to do about tomorrow tomorrow," he said, taking his turn at changing the subject.

"Fine. Be that way. I've got to get ready for work." With a shake of her head, Jade took her coffee and left the room. "I'll see you this evening," she called as she walked down the hall.

After reaching her bedroom, Jade flopped back on her bed and groaned aloud. He hadn't been in her house twenty-four hours and she was already a mess. Hopefully, he was as good a detective as he was at being alluring and irritating. He'd have the answers about her birth in no time and she could get him out of her house and move on with her life. Not that she had much of one, but it was hers and she was in control of it.

She looked over at the clock and realized she had to get a start on her day. That meant a shower. And after that chat with Harley, it would be a cold one.

"Well, well, well. Mr. Jeffries didn't warn me that he was having a meeting with Mr. Tall, Dark and Handsome today."

A sassy woman with dark, curly hair greeted Harley as he approached the receptionist's desk. She was wearing a hot pink sweater and earrings just as brightly colored, although they were hidden within the complicated ringlets of her hair. She smiled widely, turning her full attention to him as he approached her.

Harley was startled by the woman's bold assessment, but he tried to smile and pass it off. She appeared to be in her late fifties, and older women especially loved to flirt with him. He usually played along to give them a little boost to their day. He'd found that being sweet to the ladies could make or break an investigation. They'd trip over themselves to help him get what he needed.

"I usually just go by Harley Dalton," he quipped.

She looked over at her computer and nodded. "Have a seat, Mr. Dalton, and Mr. Jeffries will be with you momentarily. Can I get you coffee or something?"

"No, thank you, Mrs. White," he said, reading the placard on her desk as he settled into his seat.

"Oh, it's *Ms.* White," she clarified. "Although you can just call me Tina, sugar."

Harley sat up straight in his chair and hoped that Mr. Jeffries would hurry. Because Tina meant business.

Thankfully, before long the door opened and

a man he presumed was Mr. Jeffries stepped out. "Good morning. Come in, Mr. Dalton."

He got up quickly, shaking the man's hand and following him through the door. Before disappearing into the room, he gave a quick glance over his shoulder to confirm that Tina wouldn't be joining them. He got a sassy wink from her, but she stayed in her seat.

As the door closed and the man gestured him toward a guest chair, Harley took a deep breath, then said, "Thanks for seeing me this morning."

"I'm sorry it's taken me this long to sit down with you. I've been tied up with other matters, but you know how that goes. Thanks for taking this case and handling it personally. I know you grew up in the area. I read all about that kidnapping case in the news not too long ago, and when we decided we needed outside help, your company was the first to come to mind. Like any hospital, we have our share of claims and malpractice suits, but this was different. Babies don't get switched around every day, you know."

Harley just nodded and let the man talk. "Hopefully, it won't take long to find out what happened," he said eventually.

"We've set up an office for you here, just down the hallway," Jeffries explained. "I've had all the records from that time brought down from the archives and put in there for you to go through. If you need anything, just let Tina know. I've instructed her to make you comfortable and give you whatever you might need."

Harley nodded, suppressing a smirk. Jeffries's admin assistant had taken the orders to heart.

"Is there anything else I can do to help you get your investigation started?"

Harley flipped through his notes, underlining something he'd written earlier. "Who was the CEO of the hospital back then? I'd like to talk to him or her if I can."

"That was Orson Tate. A helluva guy. I'm sure he'll be happy to speak with you." Mr. Jeffries reached to his phone and pressed the intercom button. "Tina, can you please pull the contact information for Orson Tate? Mr. Dalton will need it." He released the button. "Anything else I can do to get you started?"

"Actually, I do have one last question before I go, Mr. Jeffries."

"Please, call me Weston."

"Very well. I've spoken with Ms. Nolan and it seems she's been receiving threats in the mail, trying to scare her into dropping the case. You wouldn't know anything about that, would you?"

Weston's eyes widened in surprise, but his gaze didn't flicker from Harley's. "I don't. I'm sorry to hear that. I sincerely hope you don't think anyone at St. Francis is behind the threats."

It was clear the man knew nothing about it. "Thank you for your time, Weston." Harley stood, shook his hand and headed out of the office.

As expected, Tina was waiting there with the former CEO's contact information and a wide smile. "I'll be right here if you need anything else, sugar."

He smiled back and quickly made his way down the hall to settle into his investigation. St. Francis's staff had faxed him some paperwork to review before he came to town, but the proprietary hospital and personnel files had to be reviewed in person. In the office, he found three large file boxes on the desk. He'd hoped there would be some video surveillance tapes as well, but it didn't take long for him to realize why there weren't.

A quick review of the security schematics from 1989 was revealing and unhelpful. Unfortunately, hospital security was not as good as it was now. While each floor had had cameras, the tapes filmed over themselves every twenty-four hours. If there ever was video evidence of someone switching the infants, it had been almost immediately destroyed. And that was if the cameras were even on. The hospital had been running on emergency power after the storm. Cameras weren't nearly as critical as life support equipment.

Specific security measures for the maternity floor weren't any better. The infants had had identification bands that matched them to their parents, but there were no alarms or tracking protocols in place to keep someone from leaving with a child or removing a band. It was possible that the bands got mixed up and put on the wrong babies to begin with. Or if they were correct, anyone with access to the nursery could've gone in and swapped the babies in their beds. It would've taken seconds to move them and switch their identification bracelets. During the storm, who would be focused on such a thing?

It was a good question. Who would've taken the opportunity to do something like that when people's lives were in danger? The ID bands weren't about to fall off the babies and they weren't removed for any reason until the babies were discharged with their parents. That meant it probably wasn't a mistake. Someone had done it deliberately, but why? Looking at the boxes, Harley was certain the answer was in there. He just had to know what he was looking for.

Settling in with a large coffee he got from the cafeteria, Harley dug into his work, taking detailed notes. After a few hours, his eyes were going out of focus, but he had a solid handle on the situation. At least, he had a handle on who Jade's biological parents might be. He was thankful, because there wasn't enough coffee to keep him awake for another hour of flipping through files.

Despite being paid by the hospital to find out what had happened, the moment he'd laid eyes on Jade his priorities had shifted. Yes, he wanted to find the truth and who was behind it, but for her, not for the money. The look in her eyes when she'd told him about never fitting in had nearly crushed him. He didn't know if finding her real family would give her the peace of mind or the sense of home she was searching for, but he was going to do his damnedest to try. He wasn't able to make her happy back then, but maybe he could now.

There were only five baby girls in the hospital at the time of the storm. Thankfully, the window Jade's parents had given him was narrow. Five was a manageable number.

He copied down the names, addresses and phone numbers on file—which were from the late eighties—hoping to make contact and potentially pay the families a visit. Ideally, he'd like to get DNA samples to eliminate the other girls. Although he envisioned them in his mind as infants, they weren't girls, they were grown women now. Likely with families of their own. And one of them had no idea her birth parents were out there somewhere, wondering what had become of her.

Harley got on his computer and sent the names to his right-hand man, Isaiah Fuller, at his office in DC. The odds of all those people being at their old addresses with the same phone numbers were slim. His research team could look up the families in various databases and records, and provide more current contact information. That wouldn't take long.

Then he could reach out and start putting faces to the names.

By the time the weekend came to a close, he could very well be on his way to knowing who Jade's real parents were. The remaining question of why the babies had been swapped, and by whom, might take quite a bit longer to nail down. It had been thirty years and he worried that the trail had gone cold long ago. But he would get to the bottom of this. For Jade's sake.

Six

Jade wasn't used to coming home to someone, but when she pulled into her driveway, Harley's Jaguar was already there. Seeing it evoked an odd sort of feeling, a sense of home the little cottage hadn't really had before. At the same time, her little car seemed a bit dowdy beside the luxury sports car. Sort of how Jade felt beside Harley. At one time, both she and her little four-door sedan had been stylish and desirable in their own way. Now they both had a lot of miles on the engine and dings in the paint job.

And yet no matter how many different ways she'd tried to run through the scenario in her mind from the night before, Harley had been eager to give her a test drive. At least at first. Then he'd run for the living room sofa, and any chance of igniting something between them had seemed like a fantasy.

It was just as well. Sophie might think that a hookup was the best thing for Harley and her, but Jade knew better. He was like her favorite potato chip. She couldn't eat just one, or even a handful, and set them aside, sated. No, she'd keep at it until she devoured the whole bag. It was easier not to eat a single chip sometimes. Or not even keep any in the house. Unfortunately, this particular treat wouldn't leave. It was about two hundred pounds of trouble she didn't need in her life, even just for a fling.

When she went in the front door, she found the house quiet and mostly dark. She didn't think Harley had been home very long. His messenger bag and suit coat were still sitting on the armchair in the living room and a light was coming down the hallway from the bathroom. She could hear the shower running.

Tired of her stuffy work attire, Jade headed to her room, where she could change into something less itchy and more comfortable than the pale pink tweed suit she'd worn beneath her white lab coat at the pharmacy. She quickly slipped into a pair of jogging shorts and a tank top. It was winter still, but the house was warmer than usual—or she was warmer than usual—with Harley around. She followed up the change by flipping her hair back and catching the mess of white-blond strands into a high ponytail out of her face.

She was stepping into the hallway when she collided with an unexpected wall of muscle. It was Harley, wet-haired and mostly naked, coming from the bathroom. She stumbled backward from the impact and he reached out to steady her, pulling her close to him again and wrapping her in the heat of his embrace.

When she recovered and was stable on her bare feet, she found herself in quite the situation. When her gaze met his, she found his serious blue eyes watching her from beneath wet strands of hair that had fallen into his face. There was an intensity there that was different than when they kissed. It wasn't even like when he'd become incensed by her threatening letter. Harley was focused one hundred percent on her in a way that made her heart stutter and her throat go dry. He might have run off the night before, but he didn't seem to be wrestling with his attraction to her now.

Unable to take it any longer, Jade broke away from his gaze and looked down to where her palms were pressed against the damp, bare skin of his chest. She could feel the rough curls of his chest hair that had intrigued her when she'd seen him in his briefs on the collapsed sofa bed. There was also a sprinkling of scars she hadn't noticed before.

Cuts, surgical scars, even what looked like a bullet wound. He hadn't mentioned much about his time in the military, but it was obvious he hadn't sat safely on an aircraft carrier, swabbing the decks.

Not that she'd ever expected him to. Harley was the kind that would jump first from an airplane. Kick down the doors of suspected terrorists. He loved the rush, which was probably why he'd made a career in this business. It was an element of his personality that had worried her just as much as a teenager as it did now. She wanted to be with someone who would come home every night, not leave her wondering if tonight was *the* night she'd get the call she dreaded.

Jade's thoughts were derailed by the stirring of Harley's desire. Her cotton shorts were slightly moist from colliding with the bath towel he had slung low around his hips. Even with the multiple layers of fabric between them, she could feel his need for her pressing against her stomach. Any questions she had about him wanting her were put to bed instantly. The bigger question now was whether she could allow herself to want him. And if so, could she manage to indulge without emotionally compromising herself? She wasn't sure.

"I'm sorry," she said at last, trying to move back and break the connection between them. Jade didn't get far. Mostly because Harley still had his arms around her waist.

"I'm not," he replied in a dead-serious tone.

Jade stiffened. She wasn't sure what to say. Was she brave enough in the moment to take what she needed? She did want Harley, even if she couldn't keep him. She wanted to feel what it was like to have someone desire her again. It was plain to her that he did. She needed to heed Sophie's advice and just go for it.

She looked into his eyes, gathering every ounce of courage and seduction she had inside her. Then she slid one palm down his chest and over the hard muscles of his stomach. She could feel him tense and quiver beneath her touch as she reached for the edge of the towel. They were both holding their breath until, with a quick flick of her finger and thumb, the white terry cloth pooled on the floor at their feet.

Harley's serious expression softened slightly as a devious smile curled his lips. "I don't think you're sorry, either," he said.

She wet her lips with her tongue and shook her head slightly. "You're right. I'm only sorry it took this long." Then she figuratively jumped in with both feet and kissed him.

The floodgates opened the minute their lips touched. All the reasons they'd had to stay away from one another went out the window as desire trumped their good sense. Jade clung to his neck, trying to draw his mouth closer to hers even as he towered over her. His hands roamed her body, reacquainting themselves with the long-denied landscape.

Jade was overwhelmed with the sensations that coursed through her. She was barely aware of their movements as Harley guided them backward into her bedroom, until she felt the mattress press into the back of her thighs.

This was really going to happen. For a moment, she almost felt eighteen again, and as if she was giving herself to Harley for the first time. A surge of nervous energy ran through her body as he slipped her tank top over her head and threw it onto her bedroom floor. She'd been so wrapped up in him back then, and the feeling was similar now. He was the bad boy, the handsome rogue who wanted her when it felt like the rest of the world didn't. There was no way her teenage self could have resisted those charms. She'd fallen head over heels.

This time was different, though. She was no enamored virgin with naive expectations about the future. She might not feel like she fitted in any more now than she did then, but Jade was a grown woman and knew that this wasn't the way to solve that problem. She was simply a woman with needs that a man like Harley could fulfill if she let him.

"Damn," he whispered in a low, gravelly voice as he looked down at her breasts. She'd always been self-conscious about them, or really, the lack of them, but he didn't seem to mind. He cupped them in his palms, sending Jade's head back as she gasped. They were small, but extremely sensitive. Her nipples turned to hard pebbles beneath his touch, aching for his mouth to taste them.

Jade eased backward onto the bed, shifting across the mattress as Harley's naked body moved forward. In an instant, he was covering every inch of her with his heated, damp skin. His desire pressed against her bare thigh as he rested on his elbows and continued to tease her nipples with his tongue until she arched her spine and pressed her hips against him.

She couldn't remember how long it had been since she'd wanted a man this badly. Had she ever? Even her attraction to Harley when they were teenagers couldn't measure up to this. They had been kids then. Now he was a man. A solid wall of man that a woman like her desperately craved.

Harley pulled away long enough to grasp the waistband of her shorts and tug them down over her hips, along with her thin cotton panties. As they reached her ankles, she kicked them off and drew up one knee to hook around his bare thigh.

"Do you have protection?" she asked. It was a little late for a question like that, but she hadn't exactly come home from work expecting this to happen.

"My gun is in the other room," he replied, with a deadpan expression on his face.

Jade smacked him on the shoulder. "You know full well what I mean. Condoms."

He grinned. "Yes, I do." Harley pulled away from her, obviously admiring every bare inch of her body as he revealed it. Then he crossed the hallway to the guest room, where he'd left his luggage.

Seconds later he returned with a fistful of gold foil packets. "Feeling ambitious?" she asked, as he tossed them onto the dresser beside the bed.

"I'm feeling like I've got a few years of making up to do." Harley reached for one and dropped it next to her on the mattress. "I also need to make up for the subpar lovemaking I offered you when we were teenagers. My form has improved greatly since then."

Jade smiled. She expected—even fantasized—that sex with Harley would be hot and frantic, but she was amazed to find that lying here with him was more comfortable than anything else. Laughter and desire blended together in a way she never could've expected. That was even better than some frenzied rush to the finish line. Jade was certain the frenzy would come soon enough, but it was nice to enjoy this moment, as well.

"Has it, now?" she teased.

Harley arched a brow. "Was that a challenge?"

She shrugged her shoulders and lay back against the mattress. "Make of it what you will."

He didn't answer. Instead, she felt his hand dip between her thighs and spread them apart. His focused gaze never left hers as his fingers sought out her center. She gasped as he gently brushed over her sensitive parts, teasing her by never fully touching her where she desired it the most. Then, when she couldn't stand it a moment longer, he stroked her hard and her body arched up off the bed.

Jade gasped and writhed, tensed and squirmed beneath his touch. He dipped his fingers inside her, rubbing the heel of his palm against her clit in a motion that made her every nerve ending light up. Within seconds of him stroking her that way, she could feel her long-denied release building up inside.

"So close," she said between short breaths.

"That's it," he coaxed. "Let go, baby."

Jade didn't have much choice. With another stroke of his palm, her orgasm exploded through her body. She was rocked by the intensity of it, as though the last few years without a lover had built up inside and burst from her all at once.

This was one of Harley's new moves and she approved.

Even as she lay on the bed, her whole body almost liquid, she reached out for him. Her fingers curled around the firm heat of his desire and slowly stroked him from base to tip. She didn't have a lot more experience to show off from their time apart, but she remembered how he liked to be touched.

Nothing had changed there. Within seconds of her touching him, Harley pulled away with a curse. That meant she was doing everything right. He grabbed the condom on the bed and sheathed himself.

Jade welcomed him with open arms as he covered her body with his own. They fitted together perfectly, each of her curves molding to his hard angles. When he filled her, that fitted perfectly, too. She drew her legs up, letting him go deeper, and clung to his back with sharp nails that dug into his skin the harder he thrust.

The closer he got to his undoing, the tighter he held Jade against him. His fingertips eventually slipped through the strands of her hair, grasping a fistful at the base of her scalp. The grip was gentle but firm, tugging her head back and exposing her throat to him. She whimpered, teetering on the edge of pleasure and pain, but realizing that the harder he pulled, the closer she came to losing control once again.

His teeth grazed her throat and she could feel the vibration of a growl from deep inside him. "Harder," she whispered, and it seemed to be exactly what he needed to hear.

His grip on her hair tightened, holding her perfectly still as he thrust into her with everything he had. The combination put Jade over the edge and the spasms of her orgasm brought on Harley's own release. With a loud groan, he thrust into her one last time, and it was done. He collapsed against her, his face buried in her shoulder for a moment before he rolled onto his back and away from her.

Jade let her body relax into the bed and took a deep breath. Even then, her mind was spinning. That was unexpected. The whole thing. And now that it was over, she wasn't sure what to do. Cuddle? Nap? Get up and make dinner? Thank him for the orgasms and put her clothes back on? She'd never had a fling before, so she wasn't quite sure what came next.

Without a better option, she pressed a kiss to Harley's cheek, rolled out of bed and went to take a shower. Maybe the hot water and breathing room would clear her mind and she could figure out the path forward.

If she was honest, the path would probably lead right back into bed with him.

Harley was confused.

Sex had rarely been a complicated thing in his mind. It was a physical release, a meeting of desires, nothing more. And that was what it was supposed to be with Jade. That's what he'd told himself, at least. But things always seemed to be more complex when Jade was involved. At least it was this time. He didn't recall it being like this the first time. There had been emotions involved back then. Puppy love, he supposed.

That was a long time ago. Things were different now. They were both mature and there was an unspoken understanding that this tryst had a time limit. He would conclude his investigation and go back to DC. She would find her family and move on with her new life. This temporary connection should be simple and enjoyable, without a bunch of expectations and romantic notions.

But now, it was the decided lack of emotions from Jade that bothered him.

It wasn't that she was disengaged or not attracted to him. The opposite was true. She had blossomed into an enthusiastic and skilled lover over the years. He tried not to think too hard about where she'd learned some of the things she'd done to him the night before. It made him want to drive to the prison just so he could punch Lance in the face.

No, what bothered Harley was the wall. Jade was physically closer to him than she had ever been, but more closed off than ever before. He supposed he should be relieved that she didn't get too attached to him too quickly, but the opposite reaction was unnerving and very unlike his Jade. The girl he remembered was an emotional open book. So full of love, so trusting.

This Jade was older, harder, less willing to open up to him or anyone else, he'd wager. It wasn't something he'd done, either. It had to be Lance. That guy had taken her innocence and stomped all over it. After going through all that, perhaps she didn't have the right head space for anything beyond the physical.

Maybe despite everything, Harley was still not good enough for her. Perhaps he would do better to focus on his case than to focus on his ex. That was what he was getting paid to do, after all.

A familiar ring tone roused him from his thoughts. It was Isaiah. Harley had been expecting this call, although he hadn't been expecting it this early in the morning. Then again, Isaiah knew what hours he kept.

He reached for his phone. "This is Dalton."

"Hey, bro," he answered in a chipper voice, despite it being five in the morning.

Harley chuckled. While technically his employee, Isaiah was more his friend than anything. He kept things sailing smoothly for him. "Good morning."

"So, I got your email about the equipment install and the list of people to run through the database. I've got good news and bad news. How do you want it?"

Harley bit back a groan. "Bad news first. Always bad news first."

"Okay. We're out of stock on a few items we need to install at the Charleston residence, so I'm afraid I won't be able to send someone down right away."

Damn it. "How long are we talking?"

"Just a few days. Maybe Monday. It depends on how quickly we can get our hands on it all."

Since Harley was staying with Jade, he supposed a delay wasn't the end of the world, but he still didn't like it. What if this had been a paying client? Or someone without a security detail to keep her safe while they waited on some video camera to be in stock? "Okay. But I want you to have a chat with inventory control. We should never be out. We should have a backup for our backups. Got it?"

"Roger that."

"And what's the good news?"

"That I have your list of addresses for all the parents and most of the daughters."

"Excellent. Email them to me."

"Already done. Check your in-box."

Harley pulled the phone from his ear and noticed the new-message alert. He opened the email and scanned through the list of names and addresses. It was incomplete, as Isaiah had mentioned. The daughter of the Steele family wasn't there. "What about Morgan Steele? She's not on here."

"I told you I had most of the daughters. She's my exception. It's going to take a little more work for her. Morgan's last known physical address was in Charleston with her parents, but that was before she went to college. After that, all I could get was a PO box at the University of South Carolina."

Harley frowned. "I doubt she's still in college."

"Correct. School records show she graduated several years back. She's likely got nothing in her name to trace. The Steele family is rich beyond belief, with multiple houses and investment properties. I'd bet she's living in a property owned by her father's trust or beneath their corporate umbrella. She probably has corporate credit cards and offshore accounts."

"What, no driver's license?"

"She has one, but it lists the family home as her address. My research shows she works at the DC facility for the family company, so I'll probably be able to get her contact information from there. Just give me a day or two."

"Steele. Why do I know that name?" Harley asked. He'd copied down the names from the hospital files, but hadn't done any research of his own yet.

"It sounded familiar to me, too, so I started doing a little research on them. The family founded Steele Tools, man. Apparently it was started in Charleston over a hundred years ago by their great-great-grandfather. They started off selling through catalogs and now they're in every home improvement store in the country. The Steele family is one of the wealthiest and most powerful in South Carolina. Or dare I say, America. They've spawned their share of CEOs, but also a senator, a judge, doctors, lawyers…you name it. Morgan works for the company, as do most of the people in the family."

The longer Isaiah spoke, the more Harley's stomach started to ache. He'd had no idea his list of candidates included such a high-profile family. Swapping babies started to make a little more sense now. Well, at least why one of the families might be targeted. Once you were that well-known, you were the focus of every crazy who wanted a piece of what you had.

"I need you to find out everything you can about the Steele family, especially over the last forty years. Any little detail could be important."

"A family like that is going to be in the papers every time one of them takes a big crap."

"I don't care. I want it all. Get your guys on it. Especially focus on Morgan Steele. If she's our girl, I want to know as much as I can about her. And get those parts we need for the surveillance system down here. I can't watch this house every second."

"Sir, yes, sir," Isaiah said sharply, with an edge of sarcasm. He would do it, though. Harley could always count on his operations manager to get things done. "Just one last question and I'll get right on it."

"Yeah?"

"What are you really doing down there, Harley?"

And with that, they'd just transitioned from employer-employee to friends chatting on the phone. "I'm investigating a case. What do you mean, what am I doing here?" he asked, knowing full well what his friend meant.

"I *mean*, since when does the CEO cart his ass down to Charleston for a piddly little case like this?"

"When the CEO gets tired of paper-pushing. And this isn't a piddly case, Isaiah. If this links back to the Steele family, it could become a very high-profile job."

There were a few moments of silence on the line before Isaiah responded again. "Cut the crap, man. Who is this woman? Tell me you'd still be down there if it were anyone else."

Harley couldn't, and they both knew it. He wasn't one to lie—he preferred avoiding the truth, which wasn't quite the same thing—and he wasn't going to lie to his best friend. He'd tell him. He just might not tell him everything. "She's my ex-girlfriend from back before I joined the navy."

"I knew it!" Isaiah shouted into the phone. "I knew there was more to it. So, what, you still carrying a torch for her or something?"

"Please," Harley said. "Have you seen me moon over a woman in the years you've known me?"

He was hardly the kind of guy who got wrapped up in a relationship, much less pine for someone. He honestly couldn't say that he'd had something that even looked like a relationship since he'd been out of the service. He hadn't had the time, the energy or the inclination. And even if he did, he hadn't met anyone who made him want more than just a little physical pleasure.

At least until he woke up this morning feeling used for the first time in his life. How the tables had turned when he least expected it…

"No. You're pretty cool and collected when it comes to the ladies. Too cool, if you ask me."

"I didn't."

Isaiah chuckled into the phone. "You're a little snippier than usual this morning."

"I'm not snippy," Harley said, knowing full well that was *exactly* the word for his tone of voice. "I'm just not in the mood for you to philosophize about my love life. It's too damn early. Yes, I was curious about Jade and what had become of her. Yes, I'm trying to do her a favor by finding out what happened to her and keeping her safe in the meantime. But that's all there is to it."

"So you're not sleeping with her?"

Harley sputtered for a moment, knowing that

even when he got his words together, Isaiah wouldn't believe him. "And if I were?" he asked at last.

Isaiah sighed heavily into the receiver and Harley could almost picture him with his feet propped up on the desk as he leaned back almost too far in his executive chair.

"I'd say there's way more to this story than you're letting on."

Seven

"Yes, I'd like to leave another message for Mr. Steele. Please press upon him the importance of my call. It's about his daughter, Morgan. Yes, it's Harley Dalton with Dalton Security calling again. I'm working on a case with St. Francis Hospital and it's imperative that I speak with Mr. or Mrs. Steele as soon as possible about a private matter."

Harley clicked off with more force than was necessary to terminate a call on a smartphone, and chucked it onto the dashboard of his car. There just wasn't the same satisfaction as slamming down an old landline phone. He needed some kind of outlet for his frustration. It was the sixth call he'd made to the Steele family's various numbers over the last three days and all he'd managed to reach were assistants or housekeepers. With them dodging his calls, all he could do now was slip his phone into his pocket and carry on with the last of his interviews.

He should've felt some sense of accomplishment by the time Sunday rolled around, but he didn't. He blamed Isaiah and his relationship meddling for that. All weekend, his friend's words had made him feel off-kilter for some reason, as though he had some kind of mental vertigo. It made him want to question his own justifications behind this investigation and why he was here in Charleston. He could've sent anyone; his friend was right. But Harley had told him to mind his own business and had got off the phone.

Now, days later, he didn't have a better answer. He just didn't know. And lately, he had too many other things to worry about.

Not that he hadn't made significant headway in the investigation over the last few days—he had. With the contact information he received from Isaiah, he'd called all the families, talking to some and leaving messages with others. With the local families he could reach, he'd set up appointments to meet with them at various times over the weekend. He'd been able to talk to every family but the Steeles so far. That didn't surprise him, but it did raise his suspicions about the wealthy family. Once he finished what he had on his plate for the day, he intended to follow up on them.

With his interviews keeping him away from the house, he'd had to figure out what to do with Jade. Since she didn't work that Friday or Sunday, he had to factor her into his plans. He scheduled as much as he could while she was working on Saturday, but there was only so much he could do then. In an abundance of caution she felt was unnecessary, he'd insisted that she spend Friday and Sunday afternoons with her parents. She had grumbled at first, suggested going with him—and then finally relented. With Jade's well-being taken care of for the afternoons, Harley was finally able to conduct his interviews in person.

Each family visit had gone the same way: he'd interviewed the parents, spoken with the daughters if possible, and taken DNA samples from anyone he could. He wasn't about to rely on clues like physical resemblance to the Nolans. Genetics were a funny thing, with recessive traits playing tricks on your eyes. Just because someone did or didn't look like their parents wasn't enough for Harley. He wanted the DNA report in hand to prove without a doubt that they shared enough genetic markers to be parent and child.

Though if asked off the record, Harley would admit all the families he'd met with today could be eliminated. Not a single person he saw had the large doe eyes he'd fallen for back in high school. By process of elimination, that left just the elusive

Steele family. He was hoping that wouldn't be the case, but the minute Isaiah had mentioned how rich and powerful they were, Harley's instincts had told him that was the path he needed to follow. The most difficult path, of course. To the family who hadn't returned his calls. With the daughter who left barely any trace of her existence.

Even then, he'd wait for the DNA reports before he shared that information with anyone. He'd had the collection of samples overnighted to his lab, and then went to see the former head of the hospital, to talk about the facility back in the nineties.

That's where he was now—sitting in the driveway outside the mansion of former St. Francis Hospital CEO Orson Tate. He killed the engine of the Jag and walked up to the front door.

It was an impressive home, filled with all the charm a traditional Charleston home should have, but few could afford. It wasn't an historical landmark, but a new building with classic details, bordering the golf course behind it. Harley rang the doorbell and waited a few moments before Orson Tate answered. He had a full head of white hair, and was wearing bifocals and a sweater.

"Mr. Dalton?" he asked.

"Yes, sir."

"Come on in," the older man said, gesturing inside as he stepped out of the doorway.

Harley shook his hand after he closed the door

behind them. "Thank you for taking the time to speak with me today, Mr. Tate."

"Oh, I've got plenty of time. I can't play golf every day. At least that's what my wife tells me. Come this way. We can chat out in the sunroom. My wife put out some tea and cookies for us."

He followed the man through the house and out a pair of French doors to a sunroom that overlooked the golf course. His prized view included a water hazard with a fountain that attracted cranes and other wildlife. Harley could see a group of golfers out on the course, laughing and playing the nearby hole.

The two of them settled into a pair of white wicker patio chairs with a platter of sweet iced tea and sugar cookies between them. Harley took out his phone to record the conversation, as he always did, and got started on their chat.

"So what's this all about, Dalton?" Tate asked as he took a sip of his tea and sat back in the cushions with a weary sigh. "Jeffries didn't tell me much on the phone, just that you would be in touch."

Harley imagined that the current CEO wanted as few people as possible to know about the situation. "Mr. Jeffries hired me to look into allegations that babies were switched at the hospital back in 1989. Specifically during Hurricane Hugo."

Orson winced and shook his head sadly. "That was a hell of a thing. Absolute chaos. I like to think we ran a pretty tight ship at St. Francis, but if something was going to go awry, that would've been the time for it. We were so close to the coast we got hit hard. It was all hands on deck. Even I was giving out water and helping nurses in triage. You know it's bad when that happens."

He could only imagine. Harley had been just a few months old at the time, with no memories of the storm, but his mother had spoken about it from time to time. Everyone in Charleston did. You didn't even have to say hurricane. It was just Hugo, like some beast had come ashore and ravished the town.

"Mr. Jeffries gave me access to all the files. There wasn't much in terms of security in place back then, at least not that survived the last thirty years. Even then, I can't help but think it would've had to have been an inside job. Perhaps one of the doctors or nurses working the floor. They were the only individuals who would've had access to the babies."

The older man nodded thoughtfully. "We considered our technology to be state of the art back then, but it's nothing compared to now. They damn near put a GPS tracker in their diapers these days. I hate to think one of our staff might have been involved in something like that, but you're right. It's that or gross incompetence, and I can't imagine how that could happen. The babies each had name bands that matched them to their parents. The bands stayed on through baths, treatments, even surgery if it was needed. You had to practically cut them off the baby's leg when they were discharged. They did not slip off. Never."

That confirmed Harley's suspicions that someone had deliberately done it. He couldn't imagine how it would happen otherwise. That meant it was time to dive into the staff's backgrounds. "I reviewed the personnel files for everyone who was working in the maternity ward during the storm." Harley reached into his bag and pulled out copies of photos taken for their hospital ID cards. He handed them over to Orson. "I don't expect you to remember every employee that worked at the hospital, but I was hoping maybe you might remember something about them that might help the investigation."

Orson flipped through the photos, studying each one thoroughly. "Dr. Parsons and Dr. Ward. Two great physicians. Never saw them lose their cool even under unimaginable stress." He turned over a photo of a nurse next. "Karen was one of our best. Uh… Karen Yarborough, I believe. She retired from the hospital after over forty years working labor and delivery. I remember her well. These other two, not so much. Although…" His voice trailed off as he studied the last photo. "This one stands out to me, but I don't remember why. What's her name?"

Harley glanced at the photo of the dowdy redhead. "That's Nancy Crowley," he said, flipping through his notes. "She worked at the hospital from 1987 to 1990, although only for a few months in maternity. Looks as though she left St. Francis not long after the hurricane, judging by what I wrote down."

"Ah," the older man said, tapping the picture with his finger. "I remember now. She didn't quit. I'm sorry to say it, but she killed herself. There were rumors that she had a drinking problem and some issues at home, but I can't be sure of it now."

Harley had a hard time disguising his surprise. He turned back to the notes and realized that her termination date was less than a week after the storm. "May I ask what happened?"

"She threw herself off the roof of the hospital. I had plenty of employees die during my twenty-five-year tenure, a few even committing suicide. It's high stress work, after all. But Nancy was the only one who did it on hospital property. That's hard to forget. It haunted the staff, especially the ones who found her. We had to bring in trauma counselors to help folks work through it. Her coworkers couldn't understand it. They said she was always so upbeat and friendly with the staff and the patients. If she had a drinking problem, she hid it well enough. No one suspected anything until it was too late."

Harley listened thoughtfully. It was an interesting lead to follow up with later. He'd have his team look up anything they could find on Nancy's death. The timing was too coincidental to ignore. "Did you ever hear anything else about it? Was a police investigation conducted?"

Orson nodded and handed the photos back to him. "Yeah, but it was pretty open-and-shut. The roof was restricted access. Surveillance cameras showed her going up there alone. When they spoke with her brother and her boyfriend, they all seemed pretty torn up about it. They didn't expect something like that from her, either. I guess you never can tell. Everyone has their demons."

When the alarm went off Monday morning, Jade woke up to a cold, empty bed. Harley had been there when she'd fallen asleep, but judging by the feel of the mattress beside her, he'd been awake for a while. She pulled on her robe and stumbled down the hallway to search for him.

Harley was sitting at the kitchen table, staring down at his coffee mug as though the answers to all the questions of the universe would be in there. Jade watched him curiously as she walked past him, poured her own cup of coffee and then sat at the kitchen table across from him.

"What's wrong?" she asked, skipping the morning pleasantries. He wasn't in the mood, judging by the look on his face. "Did you get any sleep?"

"Not really. I have too much to think about."

Jade understood that. When things were at their worst with Lance, she'd almost gone crazy from sleep deprivation. Every time her head touched the pillow, her brain would start spinning with worries that wouldn't let her drift off.

She hoped Harley's worries weren't about the two of them. They'd developed a comfortable, uncomplicated rhythm the last few days and had always ended up in each other's arms. She didn't want either of them overthinking that. "Hit a snag in the investigation?" she asked.

Harley looked up at her and frowned. He had been fairly close-lipped about his research so far. Jade tried to be understanding about it, but it was hard knowing he had information that might impact her life. She supposed that if it really mattered, he would tell her. There wasn't much use in telling her things before he was certain. Still, it was weird that he was going out to track down the truth about what happened to her, then coming home and engaging in idle chatter about the weather.

"You could say that," he said at last. "I've hit a roadblock I wasn't expecting."

"You've only just started. How can that be?"

"People are stubborn," Harley explained. "I've spent the entire weekend meeting with various people who might have information about what happened."

"Like who?"

"Like the couples who had daughters at St. Francis around the same time as the Nolans. Hospital staff. Anyone I can get to answer my calls, really."

Jade swallowed hard, the coffee burning in her

throat. One of the people he'd spoken to could be one of her parents. It was hard to believe, but true. "Oh," was all she could manage to say. "Any luck?"

The lines in his forehead convinced her that he was conflicted about what he'd found. "Yes and no. Have you ever heard of Steele Tools?"

Jade shrugged. "Yeah. I think I have a set of their screwdrivers. Why?"

"My team has been doing a little research on them. They're a fascinating success story that started here in Charleston, actually."

He continued talking about what he'd learned so far, but Jade wasn't really listening. While the history of Steele Tools might seem fascinating to Harley, she wasn't sure why she should care. Or why it seemed to weigh so heavily on his mind. "That's all nice, but what does that have to do with the case?"

Harley pressed his lips tightly together as though reluctant to say anymore. That was too damn bad. He'd started this conversation and he was going to finish it.

"Spill, Harley."

He sighed. "I've been able to contact and basically eliminate every family that had a baby girl at St. Francis when you were born except for one. Trevor and Patricia Steele were at the hospital and they delivered a daughter during the storm. They named her Morgan."

Morgan. Jade had always liked that name. She'd

personally never been a huge fan of Jade, but at least it was different. It suited her, she supposed, although she was beginning to wonder if that was the reason she liked Morgan better than her own name. Was that the name she was supposed to have? The one she'd been given the day she was born? Somehow thinking of the name like that made it sound foreign and odd to her ears.

"The problem is I've been unable to get in contact with them. I've left messages with all their secretaries and assistants, and they haven't called me back. It's incredibly frustrating, because I know we're close to the truth."

Jade tried to process what he was telling her. If all the other families had been eliminated, that meant the Steele couple's daughter was the only real candidate to be swapped with the Nolans'. Which would mean that Jade was…

"If I'm right about this, and I think I am, you're the daughter of billionaires, Jade."

She hesitated for a moment, staring blankly at Harley. She was waiting for the punch line. The gotcha. The bazinga. Instead, he just looked at her with his large eyes as though awaiting a bigger reaction.

"Billionaires?" she said at last.

"Yes."

She slumped down into the chair, trying to process what he'd told her. Right now, it was just supposition on his part. There was no evidence, no DNA to confirm it. But even if there were, a part of her wouldn't believe it. That kind of stuff just didn't happen. "Let me guess, I'm also the crown princess of Genovia, too."

Harley flinched. "Gen-*what*? I'm serious, Jade. I think you were switched at birth and deliberately taken away from the Steeles. It all makes sense."

"Does it?" she said, her voice beginning to sound hysterical to her own ears. "It doesn't make a damn bit of sense to me."

"No, listen. Follow this… You've been unable to understand why your parents were targeted. I don't think they were the targets. I think the Steele family was the real target. Your parents and their daughter were convenient."

"Why?"

Harley sat back in his chair and sighed. "That's the piece I haven't figured out yet. A family like that would be a prime target for a kidnapping or something like that."

"Kidnapping, sure. But what do they gain from swapping me with some other baby? Nothing."

"I know. It doesn't make any sense. I don't have all the pieces yet, but I know I'm on the right track. I feel it in my gut."

"Maybe you're just hungry," she said with a dry tone.

Harley scowled at her over his coffee. Apparently

her humor wasn't as welcome when he was stuck on a case. "You know, I thought you would be more interested in what I had to tell you, but you're treating it all like a joke. I mean, really, I shouldn't have said anything, but it seemed like you needed to know. It's a big discovery."

Jade came to his side and placed a gentle hand on his shoulder. "I know, and I'm sorry. Thank you for telling me. It's just a lot for me to think about. I didn't know what I expected when this whole process began, but I certainly wasn't planning on it involving rich people and kidnapping plots. I don't know what I'm supposed to do or think about the whole situation."

"You don't have to do anything. Just mull it over and let yourself get used to the idea. I don't want you to be blindsided when it all comes out and you've got reporters in your face asking you how it feels to be an instant billionaire."

She was grateful for the warning. Truly. But somehow being hit with news like that suddenly gave her more to worry about. Now she would fret, if the dull ache in her stomach was any indication.

Morgan Steele. That woman sounded powerful and in control of her life. The daughter of a wealthy family. The socialite heiress who was poised and polished to a shine. Jade was none of those things and couldn't imagine that she ever could be. It had to be a mistake. Harley was barking up the wrong tree.

Though when she looked up at him, she noticed

a light of determination and seriousness in his eyes. He knew he was right. So what did that mean for her?

"You don't seem very excited by the news. I think most people would love to find out that they're secretly a member of the wealthiest family in town."

Jade supposed she wasn't most people. "It just makes me worry, Harley. I've never fit in with my family as it was, and we were raised poor. How will I possibly fit into a family that's überwealthy? I don't know how to be rich. I don't know how to be an elegant, refined person. I'm going to stand out like a sore thumb and that's the last thing I wanted. I was trying to find out where I belonged."

"I don't know what you're talking about. You're beautiful, you're smart. I could put you in a ball gown and take you to any fancy party you could name and you'd fit right in."

Jade sighed and looked down at the worn wood of her kitchen table. It was a hand-me-down from her parents, as were most of the things in the house. She hadn't had many new belongings in her life. What little she'd gotten as wedding gifts years ago were worn out or gone by now. She hadn't bothered to bring much back from Virginia when she'd packed up and left her life with Lance behind.

To find out that she really was a Steele… She couldn't even imagine what it would mean for her life, but she hoped Harley was right. She wanted more than anything to fit in somewhere. Hopefully, a nice dress and a smile would do the trick.

She doubted it.

Eight

When Jade returned home from work Monday afternoon, she found Harley where'd she left him that morning—at the kitchen table surrounded by paperwork, staring intently at his laptop. He hardly looked up when she came in, not acknowledging her presence until she dropped her purse onto the chair beside him.

"How's it going?" she asked.

"It's going." He sighed and shut his laptop. "You're home early."

Jade winced at his observation and turned to look at the clock on the microwave. "Actually, I'm home later than usual. It's almost five. You've been buried in your work for hours. Have you eaten anything today?"

Harley sat up straight in the chair and put more thought than should have been necessary into the answer. "I ate some of those shortbread cookies you had in the pantry."

She sighed. "I appreciate your dedication to the case, but you need to eat. There's nothing in the house worth cooking. Are you up for going out to dinner? You need a break from all this, I think."

"Sure." Harley stood up and stretched with a loud groan. He had to have been sitting there for hours. "I was actually thinking of taking you someplace really nice for dinner tonight."

Jade stiffened where she stood. Someplace nice? She wasn't quite sure what that meant. Or what it implied. Did he mean a date? They'd had sex. Things were casual but flirtatious between them. But nothing as traditional as a date had been mentioned before. So that probably wasn't what he meant. Or did he? She groaned internally and decided to focus on what she knew for sure.

"Really nice? Are we talking Red Lobster or… I don't even know what's nice in town. A lot changed while I was living out of state."

Harley rolled his eyes. "Actually, I thought we might take the opportunity to dip your toe into a little of the fancy lifestyle you may be facing if you're a part of the Steele family. Give you a chance to be more comfortable with that sort of thing."

So, *not* a date. Jade was both disappointed and

relieved. "I think that's a little premature, but I suppose it can't hurt."

"Great. You go get ready and I'll see if I can wrangle some last-minute reservations."

Jade wandered down the hallway to her room to figure out what she was going to wear. Sorting through her closet, she eyed some choices and settled on the ever-appropriate little black dress. It was a silky fabric with lace cap sleeves and a deep V neckline that highlighted her collarbones. It had a ruched waist, giving her the appearance of an hourglass figure she didn't have, and fell right at the knee. Not too long or too short. With the right accessories and some black patent leather pumps, she hoped this dress would be suitable for any of the nicer restaurants in downtown Charleston, which she'd never visited before.

She pulled her hair back into a chignon at the base of her neck and touched up her makeup to last a few more hours. She added the pearl earrings and matching necklace her parents had given her for her wedding day—the nicest jewelry she owned—and then studied herself in the mirror.

Jade had to admit she looked lovely. Maybe as lovely as she ever had. It would probably be enough to pass at whatever restaurant Harley chose tonight. But this was just a test run. Would the woman in the mirror pass for a member of the Steele family? That was a better question.

And would it ever come to that?

When she returned to the living room, she found Harley there in a black suit with a silk, charcoal-gray shirt. He'd forgone the tie tonight and she liked it. The open collar gave just a peek of the hollow of his throat, which she was certain smelled like a mix of his cologne and the warm musk of his skin. It took everything she had to pick up her purse and not bury her face there to draw in his scent.

After seeing him around the house in more casual clothes the last few days, it was nice to see tailored and put-together Harley once again, too. He was like a chameleon, blending in to any environment. Looking at him now reminded her of the moment she'd opened the front door to find him on her porch. It was hard to believe that was only a week ago. The same butterflies took flight in her stomach when she looked at him this time, too.

He didn't seem to notice. Harley was too busy staring at her. "You look…" He cleared his throat and nodded. "You look very nice."

Jade smiled and glanced down at her ensemble. "Is this okay for where we're going?"

"Absolutely. I'm sure you'll be the most beautiful woman there tonight."

She had a hard time believing such a big compliment, but after their earlier discussion, she decided not to argue with him. He seemed to believe it, which meant it was true, at least in his eyes. "Thank you," she said.

He offered her his arm and escorted her out the door to his Jaguar.

"So where did you end up getting a reservation?" she asked as he drove out onto the highway toward downtown Charlestown.

Harley smiled, his eyes fixed on the road. "Well, I know a guy who has recently invested in a great steak house in an old converted carriage house. You're going to love it."

About twenty minutes later, they pulled up to the valet stand outside of Harrison Chophouse. While Harley handed over the keys, Jade waited patiently on the curb, reading decals on the tinted glass windows that pronounced several awards they'd won, including most romantic restaurant and top ratings from various dining and travel sites.

Inside, they found a dimly lit room made all the more intimate and warm by the dark wood paneled walls and crackling fire in the stone hearth in the center of it all. Each table had a white tablecloth, a flickering candle and a small centerpiece of fresh flowers. Most tables were occupied and a small crowd was gathered in the lobby, waiting for seats.

Harley made his way to the maître d's stand, and Jade was surprised when they were immediately escorted back to an intimate corner table. She settled into the chair across from Harley and accepted the menu that the maître d' handed her.

Her gaze had barely flicked over the selection of seafood and steaks when another man approached the table and introduced himself as the restaurant's sommelier. "May I offer you something from our extensive wine list?" he asked. "I highly recommend the 2014 Opus One, which is a lovely red blend, or the Silver Oak cabernet sauvignon."

"Do you like red wine?" Harley asked.

She nodded. "Whatever you like best," she said. In truth, she wasn't sure if she liked red wine or not. She hadn't drunk much wine in her lifetime. She occasionally had a glass of white wine at social functions, but that was about it. Especially after things went down with Lance. Somehow consuming any kind of addictive substance had made her uneasy for the first year or so. But she was willing to try whatever was appropriate for tonight. It was part of the experience, she supposed.

Harley looked over the wine list for a moment and ordered a bottle of something she couldn't pronounce. The man seemed pleased, disappearing for a few moments and returning with Harley's selection.

The sommelier went through the ritual of opening the wine and pouring a small sample for Harley to try. Once he approved, the man poured a glass for each of them and left the bottle on the table.

Jade casually picked up the wine menu and found what Harley had selected. It was a four-hundred-dollar bottle of wine, and didn't even come close to being the most expensive choice on the list.

"You'll get used to it," he said with a smile as he seemed to notice her reaction.

Jade looked at him and frowned. "Get used to what?"

"Your new life. If it turns out that you're the true Steele heiress, a lot of things are going to change. It took me a while to adjust, too, especially after spending so many years overseas. I was accustomed to living in such rough conditions that just coming back to the States was luxurious. Then once my company took off and I found I had more money than I could ever spend, it took time to adjust to a new way of looking at the world. I had always had a poor man's perspective. In some ways I still do, but I tried to broaden my horizons. If I wanted something, I could have it. I could eat at nice restaurants and wear expensive suits. I can spend more than I paid in rent money for my old apartment on a single bottle of wine. The key for me is to never take it for granted."

Jade wasn't sure if she could ever do that. "Don't you feel like an imposter?"

"Every day of my life. I thought for the longest time that people would see through it all and kick me to the curb as though I didn't belong. But it never happened. The same will happen to you, Jade. You might feel out of place, but you'll fit in soon enough. I'd say you already would fit in if you'd take a deep breath, take a sip of that ridiculously expensive wine and allow yourself to relax."

She shook her head and looked back down at the menu. "I don't know about it being that easy," she said, but forced herself to take a deep breath, anyway. "I'm not so confident that my life is going to change, Harley. Even if you get the proof you need and the Steeles turn out to be my real parents, that doesn't mean they're going to welcome me with open arms. And even if they did, I doubt they're going to give me a room in their mansion, hand me a checkbook and immediately rewrite their wills to include me. I might end up like the distant cousin that only gets invited to Christmas dinner. After all this, I'll probably live the same middle-class life I've scratched out for myself."

Jade reached for her glass and took a healthy sip. It was lovely. Better than the twelve-dollar-a-bottle stuff she was used to having from time to time, as well it should be.

It worked its magic on her quickly, however, especially on an empty stomach. The splash of cabernet warmed her and relaxed her muscles. Perhaps that was why the rich liked wine so much, she thought. It helped them deal with the stresses of their wealthy, complicated lives.

Harley looked at her across the table with exasperation in his blue eyes. "You haven't even met these people yet and you're already planning their inevitable rejection. Care to tell me why that is?"

She didn't know for sure. "I don't know what to say, Harley. I just can't buy into the fantasy. My whole life I've fought to do the right thing and make the best choices, and it always seems to fly back in my face. I don't know why this would be any different. Maybe a part of me knows that if I expect the worst, I might be pleasantly surprised for a change."

"Is that how you feel about me? About us? That if you expect all of this to end badly and it doesn't, at the very least you won't be disappointed?"

Jade narrowed her gaze at him. He was looking so handsome in his suit, even as he pressed her about unpleasant topics. She studied the lines and angles of his face for a moment as she gathered her thoughts. It was easier to focus on the broken, offset nose, the evening stubble along his jaw and the dark brown eyebrows that framed his face than on the two of them and what was going on between them.

"I don't know how you and I are going to end, Harley. But yes, there's certainly a part of me that knows better than to give too much importance to it. You're going to crack the case and go back to DC, while I stay in Charleston and work through my identity crisis. Thinking what we have is anything more than a fun indulgence to scratch that itch for old time's sake is a recipe for heartbreak, don't you think?"

He didn't answer, but studied her face intently as she spoke. Jade wasn't sure if he agreed with what she'd said or was irritated by it. Finally, he nodded and reached out to pick up his wineglass. "What shall we drink to tonight?"

Jade thought for a moment as she picked up her own. "To the future?" she suggested.

He smiled. "To the future," he replied, clinking his crystal glass gently against hers. "And being pleasantly surprised by everything it has in store for you."

"For both of us," she corrected.

They returned to a disaster area.

Harley was beyond furious as he watched Jade step gingerly through the remains of her living room in her nice dress and heels. While they were away at dinner, someone had broken in and done his best to try to scare Jade.

As she bent down with trembling hands to pick up a shattered frame containing a photograph of her family, Harley worried that perhaps whoever it was had been successful. Jade was a strong, stubborn woman, but everyone had their limits.

The cops had already come and gone, taking statements and photographs, but offering little to make Jade feel any better about her situation. As it was, the living room bore little resemblance to what they'd left behind only a few hours ago. It was the same in all the other rooms of her tiny bungalow—nothing seemed to be taken, but everything was torn apart. Overturned furniture, dumped out drawers, broken glass...even a message spray painted across her living room wall: Quit While You're Ahead.

Just looking at the sloppy red paint splattered across her beautiful little space was enough to send Harley's blood pressure skyrocketing. She'd come back to Charleston to start a new life. To rebuild after Lance destroyed everything they had together. And now, something that had happened thirty years ago was threatening this new chance. He didn't know that Jade would ever be able to live in this house alone and be comfortable. Even with all the best technology he could install.

Damn the delays. If his guys had been here days ago the way they'd planned, the house would've been rigged with cameras rolling to catch the intruder as he approached. The system would have protected the house, and more importantly, protected Jade's feelings of security. She'd argued with him that her neighborhood was safe and she didn't need all that equipment. He doubted she would argue with him about it now.

"I don't understand," Jade said, as she dropped the photograph back to the floor and sat down on the couch. "Why would someone do something like this?"

"To rattle you," Harley replied. "If this is the same person who wrote the note, and I think it is, he's escalating their threats. You haven't dropped the case, so they wanted you to know they're serious."

"But who cares?" she lamented. "Why would someone be so invested in me not finding my family? I'm no Princess Anastasia."

He shook his head and moved to sit beside her. "If we uncover the motivation, we may very well find out what happened to you as a baby and why. Whoever was involved doesn't want the truth coming out. You're just the driving force behind the investigation, and therefore, the target of their aggression. Simple as that."

"Simple as that," Jade parroted with a flat tone and dead eyes that focused on the spray-painted threat.

Harley didn't like seeing her that way. It wasn't like his Jade. She was a fighter, and this bastard had broken her. Harley's hands curled into fists in his lap as he looked around at the mess. He felt helpless, something he almost never was. He always had something he could do to correct a situation. He wanted to beat the person responsible to a pulp, or drop them into the world's worst prison, where they'd never be heard from again.

But for now, he needed to figure out what he could do to help.

As he was thinking, Jade leaned against him and laid her head on his shoulder. She wrapped her arms around his biceps and held him tightly. "I'm glad you're here," she said. "If I had come home alone to find this, I don't know what I would've done."

She was right. At least he was here with her. She wasn't going through all of this alone. He was glad he'd followed his instincts when she'd received that threatening letter. Jade hadn't been happy about him imposing on her life, but it had been the right choice.

He turned to bury his face in the white-blond strands of her hair, and breathed in the scent of her shampoo. The familiar and fruity smell helped him relax, letting the knotted muscles in his neck and shoulders unwind. He didn't need to prepare for battle. At least not tonight.

"I'm glad I was here, too. I'm going to find out who's doing this to you, Jade, and I'll make sure they can't hurt you ever again."

She didn't respond, just clung more tightly to his arm. He'd hoped that he would get a chance to hold her again tonight, but this wasn't what he'd had in mind. The mood was definitely shattered, along with most of her things.

Jade said she would call her insurance company in the morning, but he knew they would do only so much. He would phone the office and have his assistant set up a cleaning crew to get the place put back together, while his team installed the security equipment that had arrived a day too late.

But in the meantime…

"Jade, pack a bag. We're leaving."

She snapped out of her sad fog and sat up, turning to look at him with confusion furrowing her brow. "What?"

"This place isn't safe any longer. We're not staying here tonight."

"Where are we going to go?"

Harley thought about it for a moment, firming up the plans in his mind. "We're going to my mother's house."

"I don't know, Harley. That would be weird. I don't want her getting the wrong idea about us."

"She won't."

"I don't want to impose."

Harley sighed and crossed his arms over his chest. Why was everything an argument with Jade? "You won't be imposing. My mother's house is huge. I paid for it. I pay someone to clean it. If you tried hard enough, she might not even know you were there."

"We can't just get a hotel room here in town?"

"No. I was staying with her until I came here. And now, so are you."

"But…"

"No buts. The threats are getting more serious,

Jade. The only way to end them is to complete the investigation. I can't do that and also protect you every minute of the day. My mother's house is an old plantation property surrounded by twelve acres of wooded wetlands. It's gated, alarmed, surveilled and completely secure. It's a damn fortress with arches and columns. That's the only place I would feel comfortable leaving you right now. I'm not even sure I want you to work for the next few days. You're too exposed to the public there."

Jade took a deep breath, and as she let it out, he could see the fight draining out of her, too. "Okay. I'll call in sick for a couple days. How much should I pack?"

He didn't want to say it out loud, but he couldn't see Jade living here again, so everything? "At least enough clothing and toiletries to get you through two or three days. We can always come back and get more if we need to."

"More than three days?"

Harley shrugged. "It all depends on my investigation. Until we know the truth, and the person responsible for this is in jail, I don't know where else you can stay. They'd just trace you to your parents' house. No one will know you're with me, or where my mother lives. She's as big of a black hole of digital data as I am. They won't be able to find her."

Jade nodded and stood up to make her way to what was left of her bedroom. It should be easy to pack, with everything strewn on the floor, but he figured it would take her a while to get things together. Before she went down the hall, she stopped and turned back to Harley.

He thought she might say something. Her eyes were overflowing with emotion, but instead of speaking, she just lunged forward and wrapped her arms around him in a ferocious hug. Jade's face was buried in his neck as she clung to him. She didn't say a word, but Harley got the message loud and clear.

He hadn't wanted it to happen this way, but he'd finally brought down the wall between the two of them. The last of Jade's fortifications had fallen and she was letting him in, at last.

And he wasn't sure what he should do next.

Nine

When Harley said he'd bought his mother a plantation, Jade had been thinking it was a metaphor for a big house, or at the very least, an exaggeration. Then the iron gates opened and his Jaguar traveled down the road that led to the Rose River Mansion and she realized he was telling the truth. It was an actual 1800s-era plantation home.

Unlike the typical White House style with two-story columns, Rose River was unique in these parts. She was no architect, but *Gothic* was the only word that came to mind, even with its traditional white wood siding and copper peaked roof. Like a cross between an old chapel, a house and a European chalet, it was so detailed that Jade figured she could stare at it for hours and see something new every time she looked. It was like something out of a novel, making her little bungalow look like a shack in comparison.

As they parked and walked up the pea gravel path to the front door, she gazed at the ancient oak trees overhead, which were dripping with Spanish moss highlighted by the moonlight. Brick steps led to a grand porch with three cusped arches and clustered piers welcoming guests inside. As they climbed the stairs to the porch, however, Jade saw modern touches of Harley in the old house. There were video cameras beneath the eaves and technologically advanced locks on the front door and windows. Knowing him, the original glass had been replaced with bulletproof panes.

Instead of using a key, Harley reached out to punch in a six-digit code, then pressed his thumb on a scanner to unlock the door. It swung open and he gestured for her to go inside ahead of him.

Jade stepped into the grand entrance hall with its two-story ceiling, sparkling chandelier and spiral staircase. She couldn't imagine living someplace like this. It was quite a leap from the tiny apartment Harley had shared with his mother back in high school. She knew he had done well for himself with his business, but this was on another level.

"Is your home in DC like this?" she asked, as she studied the marble floors and intricate moldings.

Harley shut the door and dropped their bags on the floor beside him. “Not even close,” he said. “My taste runs a bit more modern. I have a three-story town house in Georgetown. It’s over a hundred years old, but you wouldn’t know it.”

“I’m sure you gutted all the charm out of it and added all your security features in the process.”

“I didn’t have to,” he stated with a smile. “The previous owner was a higher-up in the CIA. It was completely renovated and locked down tighter than the Vatican vaults when I bought it.”

“Sounds perfect for you,” she said smugly.

“Harley, is that you, dear?”

Jade turned in time to see Harley’s mother come through a set of French doors to greet them. Though she certainly looked older than when they’d last met, the years had been kind to her. She paused for a moment as she gazed at the two of them in the entry, then grinned widely.

“Jade?”

“Yes, it’s me, Mrs. Dalton.”

The woman came forward quickly, scooping Jade into a big hug. It was just like the ones she remembered from her teen years, although now his mother smelled like Chanel No. 5 and was wearing sparkling diamond studs in her ears. She finally pulled away and studied Jade for a moment. “Lovely. Just lovely.”

Then she turned to her son. “Harley Wayne Dalton, why didn't you tell me you were bringing Jade here tonight? I would've had a room prepared for her. Now the housekeeper has already gone to bed for the evening. It's past eleven."

"It was a last-minute decision, Mama. Her house was broken into and I didn't want to stay there tonight."

"Oh no, that's just awful," she said in the thick Carolina drawl Jade remembered. "Of course you're going to stay here, aren't you? Since Gabby is asleep, I'll run upstairs and get a room ready for you." She paused for a moment, looking curiously at them both with arched eyebrows. "Unless you'll just be sharing Harley's room?" she asked with a hopeful twinkle in her eyes.

"That's fine, Mama. We'll share. I told her you wouldn't go to any trouble."

Mrs. Dalton frowned in irritation, and in that moment, Jade could see she really was the female version of Harley. Her dark brown hair was pulled back, showing the silver streaks that ran through it like elegantly placed highlights. She had the same high cheekbones, the same piercing blue eyes and the same devious smile. "It's no trouble," she fussed. "I don't get company very often."

"No, really, Mrs. Dalton. Don't worry about me. At the moment, I just want to get out of these heels, find a bed and pass out on it. I'm exhausted."

"Okay," she agreed reluctantly. "Harley, why

don't you show her around and take her upstairs to your room. If you need anything, you just come and get me."

Harley nodded, picked up their bags and headed toward the grand staircase. Jade followed him, taking in the artwork and decor as they climbed the curving stairs and went down the hallway.

"My room is in the west wing of the house," he explained. "We're down here to the left."

He nudged open the door with his shoulder and stepped inside. Jade followed him into the large, bright room with its king-size bed. It had a pale blue duvet that matched the paintings on the walls. Most of the furnishings were white and oversize, but fit well within the space. There was a desk and television on the wall opposite the bed.

Harley placed both bags on the bed and then flopped down onto the mattress beside them. "The closet is there—" he gestured to a door "—and the bathroom is over there." He pointed toward a second one.

Jade kicked out of her high heels and sighed in relief as her feet sank into the plush carpeting. It had been a long, stressful evening and her body was starting to feel the effects. She peeked her head into the bathroom and found a Carrara marble palace awaiting her, with a large soaking tub and a tile-and-glass shower big enough for two.

"I think I'm going to take a bath," she said.

"Enjoy," Harley answered, as he kicked off his own shoes and reached for his laptop bag. He took out his computer, and then his handgun, which he placed on the nearby nightstand. Thankfully, all his things had been in the car with them tonight. She had no doubt that her intruder would've taken or destroyed Harley's notes and files to set back the progress of the investigation.

He still seemed preoccupied and on edge, and Jade understood. While everything that happened tonight was traumatic for her, it was different for Harley. Even if he didn't see the situation as some sort of failure on his part, which it wasn't, it was more than likely going to fire him up. He was already pouring everything he had into the investigation, but with the stakes raised, he wouldn't rest until he had the answers.

Jade closed the door to the bathroom behind her and did her best to leave her worries, and his, outside the marble oasis. She started the hot water, pouring in some rose-scented oil she found on the counter. She stripped out of her clothes and jewelry and pulled her hair up on top of her head in a messy bun before dipping in her toe and climbing into the bathtub.

She was exhausted, both emotionally and physically, and this was exactly what she wanted. Her little house offered most of the things she needed, but not a soaking tub. It made her miss the one she'd had in her house with Lance. One more thing to add to the list of things that she'd lost over the past few years.

When Jade lay back and closed her eyes, she found she couldn't relax as easily as she'd hoped. She was worried. Not about the investigation. Not really even about the break-in. Yes, there was a threat from an unknown source, but she had no doubt that Harley would do everything he could to protect her. That was actually the problem. He would do anything. That scared her.

When they'd found her home in disarray, she'd noticed something change in Harley. A switch had flipped inside him and any ideas she might have entertained about him settling into the quiet life of a CEO went out the window. He was instantly in combat mode, pushing her behind him and searching the house, pistol drawn, to make sure the culprit wasn't still there. When he was satisfied, he'd called the police and put away his weapon, but she could tell he was still wound tight.

She appreciated his efforts, but the excitement in his eyes worried her. Her bad boy from high school had always enjoyed living on the wild side. The military fed right into his need for adrenaline. His money and success might offer him fewer opportunities for adventure, but he still enjoyed the rush of danger. Jade supposed he couldn't go from jumping out of airplanes and interrogating suspected terrorists to filing paperwork, and still be fully content with his life.

She knew that much. She'd known it when she'd walked away from him all those years ago, and she knew it when she'd invited him into her bed a few days ago. That was why she'd gone into this whole situation with caution. Harley was older and wiser, but not everything had changed. The quiet, peaceful, secure life she craved was never going to be okay for a man like him.

Jade took a deep breath and tried to let the hot water and the scent of the oil relax her and chase away her anxieties. The bottom line was that keeping emotionally distant from Harley was hard, but necessary. She had enough going on in her life without dealing with the inevitable heartbreak of falling for him. Whether he ended it or she lost him in a dangerous twist of fate, she would end up alone and hurt, and she couldn't go through that again.

When the water started to go cold, she gave up on her brain winding down into relaxation and decided she needed to just go to bed. Maybe then she could get a break from her own thoughts for a while.

Wrapped in a towel, she stepped out into the bedroom and found Harley sitting at the desk with his laptop. He wasn't frowning at the screen this time, though. There was a glint of interest in his eyes that caught her attention. That was different. It made

Jade wonder what information he'd managed to uncover this late, after such a long and miserable night.

"I believe I'm going to have to think outside the box with this case," he said. "If I can't get the Steele family to contact me, I'm just going to have to go directly to them."

"What do you suggest?" Jade asked, as she unzipped her bag and pulled out something to sleep in. "I can't imagine you could just stroll up to their front door or march into their offices downtown."

"Normally, you'd be right." Harley turned his laptop around to face her.

She tugged on an oversize Clemson T-shirt from her undergraduate years and walked over for a closer look. It was the website for the annual Steele Tools charity ball, scheduled for Friday night at the Steele estate.

"Isaiah just sent me the link for this, along with more background on Morgan. This is the one night of the year that you *can* stroll right up to their door and go inside, as long as you pay for a ticket. As the community outreach representative for the company, Morgan will be at that party, I have no doubt. As will the rest of the family. All I have to do is dust off my tuxedo and lay out the required donation to get that ticket."

"You're going to look suspicious going by yourself," Jade said.

If the family had been deliberately avoiding

him, they probably had people on the lookout for attendees that didn't belong. She had no doubt he would look handsome, but a single man typically wouldn't go to a party like that alone. Especially a man who looked like Harley, fresh from the front lines. "You're going to need a date if you want any chance of getting in the front door."

Harley stopped and looked at her with conflict in his gaze. He knew she was right, she could tell, but he didn't like it. "I can't take you to the party," he said.

Jade couldn't hide her pout as she crossed her arms over her chest. "Why not? You said if you put me in a pretty dress you could take me anywhere."

"That's absolutely true. But you know I'm trying to not involve you in the case. I'll be there to ask questions and try to get an in with the Steeles. Is that really how you want to meet your potential family? Accidentally bumping into your birth mother in line at the bar?"

She hadn't thought about it that way, but the more she considered what he said, the less it mattered. "Actually, I think this might be better. It would take the pressure off to just be there and observe them, without this big announcement about me being their daughter hanging over my head."

"And you think you'll be able to keep your cool and not say anything? Pretend like they're nothing to you even as I try to corner Morgan into a private discussion? If her parents aren't cooperating, it's critical that I get her on board to help."

Jade nodded confidently. "I can. And even if I couldn't, you have to take me, Harley. You can't leave me by myself. You said yourself that it's too dangerous."

"I can leave you here. You're perfectly safe with my mother," he countered.

"Well, then who else are you going to drag to a black-tie party on such short notice?"

Finally, after she'd chipped away at all his excuses, he relented, although he still had a wary look in his eyes. "Okay, you're right. I don't have a lot of options here. I can't believe I'm about to say this, but Jade Nolan, will you go to the dance with me?"

Harley felt incredibly out of place in the department store. Like a bull in a china shop, he tried to stay in the corner and out of the way, but he was just too large a man in such a tiny dressing area. The dressing rooms themselves were down a narrow hall, but he was waiting just outside of them where a three-paneled mirror offered a view of your every angle whether you wanted to see it or not. The room was also had a small counter where a chic woman dressed all in black assisted the ladies and rehung outfits that they passed on. Every time a woman went in or out, he had to press into the wall so she could pass between him and the clerk.

"Do I have to be here for this?" he said loudly, making the clerk roll her eyes at him. He didn't care.

"Yes." Jade's voice drifted to him from over the wall partition. "You've generously offered to buy me a new gown, so should get some say in what I wear to the party."

Yeah, that's what she'd said as she lured him into the department store. After perusing rack after rack of beaded and silky gowns, Jade had led him to the dressing area so she could try on a few of the selections. Somehow the idea of seeing Jade model a bunch of slinky garments was better in his mind than it was in reality.

"Fine," he growled. He didn't understand why a place selling dresses that cost more than his first car couldn't have a bigger fitting room area. He should've just hired a personal shopper to handle this, but Jade had told him he was being silly. It was bad enough that he was buying her a dress, she'd said. Jade hadn't wanted to accept, but he'd insisted she needed something nice enough to blend in with the other rich partygoers. Since she didn't have anything suitable, she could choose between staying home or letting him buy her a dress.

Only then had she relented. But she wasn't going to let him go overboard. She'd insisted she would just pick out something off the rack, whatever that meant.

He sighed and crossed his arms over his chest.

Hopefully, one of the dresses she'd selected would work. Harley couldn't imagine going through all this a second time at another store.

"Are you going to come out in any of them?" he asked.

"As soon as I find one worth showing you, yes."

After an eternity of waiting, he finally heard a door down the corridor unlatch, and a moment later, Jade emerged from the dressing room in a crimson beaded gown. It had a plunging square neckline that highlighted the delicious curves of her small, firm breasts and her long, graceful neck. The cap sleeves left most of her arms bare, highlighting the stark contrast between her pale skin and hair and the blood-red fabric. The beaded and sequined design crisscrossed over the dress and down to the floor, where it just barely pooled at her feet.

She looked—in a word—stunning.

Harley felt his chest tighten as he stared at her. She was every bit the elegant lady he suspected she really was. She felt like she'd never fitted in, but he was certain that was only because she hadn't grown up with the family she was meant to have. Even with her blond hair up in a clip, and her feet bare, she looked ready to walk down a grand staircase into the elegant party she was about to attend.

He would be more than proud to have her on his arm. In fact, he was more than a little worried that she'd be too beautifully conspicuous for them to attend the gala unnoticed.

And he wanted to whisk her into the dressing room and violate every rule the department store had. Being escorted out by security would be worth it if he could get his hands on her at that moment.

Clearly oblivious to his thoughts, Jade examined herself in the three-way mirror and finally looked up at him with concern wrinkling her forehead. "I'm not sure about this one," she said. "What do you think?"

"I love it," he said. And he meant it.

Jade narrowed her eyes at him suspiciously. "You're just saying that because you're tired of shopping. I could come out in a trash bag and you'd be ready to buy it."

"That's not true," Harley argued. "That's hardly a trash bag. The color is beautiful on you, and the cut is very flattering."

"This is an Elie Saab," the clerk said, as she swooped in to help Jade make her choice. "He's right, it really does look lovely on you."

"See?" Harley challenged.

Jade just shook her head and turned to the mirror again. When he saw the back of the dress, he felt as though his lungs had turned to stone in his rib cage. He couldn't breathe as his gaze ran over the bare expanse of her skin and the low dip of the fabric. It begged him to run his fingertips down her spine.

He could envision them dancing at the ball together as she wore that dress. Her body pressed against his, Harley's palm flattened to her bare lower back. He hated dancing. Had no interest in it normally. But that dress could change his mind.

"I don't know," Jade said. He could still hear the doubt in her voice. "It's a pretty dress, but is this what I want to be wearing to meet what could be my family for the first time?"

Harley had been wondering if there was more to her indecision than just a fashion choice. They'd looked at twenty dresses before she chose a few to try on. Now it seemed as though they were closing in on the real issue. Jade would look lovely in anything she wore, but she wanted to make a good first impression.

With a sigh, he walked up behind her and pressed his palms into her shoulders. He looked at her through their reflection in the mirror with a sincere expression. "This party is just our chance to make first contact. We don't have to tell them who you are if you're nervous. But if they really are your family, Jade, they're going to love you no matter what you have on. Whether you wear this beautiful dress or the trash bag you mentioned earlier, they're not going to care, because you're amazing."

He watched in the mirror as Jade's eyes started to tear up. She nodded slightly and then blinked them away. "You really like this one?" she asked, with a more confident smile painted on her face.

"I do. I'd be happy to buy it for you. I'd also be very happy to help you take it off."

Jade turned to face him. "Well, if all goes well at the gala, you might just get that chance."

He wrapped his arms around her waist, seeking out the bare expanse of her back. Her skin was cool to his heated touch, making a chill run through his whole body at the contrast. He took a deep breath to wish away the surge of desire suddenly racing through his veins. "You mean after dangling this tempting fruit in front of my face, you're going to make me wait until after the Steeles' party to taste it?"

Her dark eyes were focused on his as another smile curled her lips. "You won't have to wait for a taste, but I'm not letting you mess up this dress before I even get a chance to wear it."

"I'll just have to get you naked then," he said. "To preserve the dress."

A loud "ahem" from the salesclerk distracted them both and severed the sexual tension building in the tiny dressing room lobby.

"This is the one," Harley insisted. "Ring it up."

Jade nodded and pulled away from his embrace. "I'll change and be right out." She gave him a sly wink before she rounded the corner and disappeared from sight.

Lord, he wanted that woman.

Harley had never experienced anything like it in the years they'd been apart. He'd met and wooed his share of beautiful women. Smart women. Strong women. Talented women. They were each appealing and alluring in their own ways, but not one of them held a candle to Jade. He was drawn to her on every level—chemical, physical…even on an emotional level. And it was dangerous. If he wasn't careful, he could give himself up to this pull she had on him.

And then what?

He wasn't sure. That wasn't his plan when he'd first kissed her. He'd wanted to overdose and get Jade out of his system. Instead, he'd become an eager and willing addict.

No, he wasn't sure what the future held for the two of them, but for the first time, he was anxious to find out.

Ten

The house was dark and quiet when they returned from the department store with Jade's new dress. She'd expected Mrs. Dalton to be in the living room, reading a book or watching television, but she was nowhere to be found.

Harley looked down at his phone as he flipped on the light in the entry hall. "She's gone to dinner and a movie with a man she met on OurTime.com," he said, reading her text aloud. "She says not to wait up for her."

Jade smiled. "Good for her."

He didn't seem to be as excited. "When she comes home, I'm getting the guy's information and running a background check on him."

"So suspicious," Jade noted, shifting the garment bag in her arms.

"Do you know how many cases we handle that deal with internet dating? Scammers, catfishers, missing women, false identities, stalkers, bigamists…too many to count. And that doesn't even take into consideration your run-of-the-mill jerks or perverts sending unsolicited dick pics."

Her eyes widened. If the idea of internet dating had appealed to her before, she was second-guessing it now. "I guess it's a good thing I haven't bothered to sign up for any of those sites yet."

"Good," Harley replied gruffly. "You don't need to be on there, anyway."

She turned toward him. "Why not? That's how people meet these days. I've been divorced for almost two years now. I didn't think I was ready to date yet, but maybe it's time. I'll have to ask your mom how it's going for her when she gets home."

A glint of jealousy flickered in Harley's blue eyes, and it was exactly what she'd hoped to see when she said those things. She wasn't really interested in online dating. What she wanted was for him to tell her why she didn't need to do it. That she wasn't single. That she didn't need a dating site because she had him. Perhaps that he cared for her on some level. But she knew he wouldn't. And it was foolish of her to even entertain such a thought.

For a moment, he looked as though he might

prove her wrong. Words seemed to linger on the tip of his tongue for a moment as his square jaw flexed. "You can meet plenty of guys in real life without going through all that," he added instead. "Especially when you're wearing a dress like that one."

Jade let a smug smile curl her lips. She thought she had gotten a rise out of Harley in that dressing room. He was flirty, as always, but there had been a light of appreciation in his eyes when she stepped out in the dress that she couldn't ignore. Even if she'd hated the dress she would've bought it just for the way he looked at her while she was in it.

"Speaking of which, I'm going to go hang this up, in your bedroom. Do you want to help me?"

Harley frowned. "You need help?"

Jade looked at him with the sultriest gaze she could come up with. "Well, it is an awfully big house. I don't want to get lost. And we are here all alone…"

He caught on fast. Before she could even take a step toward the staircase, Harley had scooped her up into his arms and was carrying her across the marble hall. Jade squealed in surprise, clutching the dress high in her arms to make sure it didn't trip them in catastrophic fashion.

She buried her face in his neck as he climbed the stairs. It was soothing to breathe in the scent of his skin and think about what was coming instead of pondering how painful a fall down the stairs would be. When she finally looked up, they were at the bedroom door. He kicked it open, stepped forward and gently set her down on the edge of the bed.

"What was that all about?" she asked, now that she was safely on the ground.

"You said you needed help and didn't want to get lost." He grinned. "I try to be as helpful as I can, especially when a lady is in distress."

Jade shook her head. "You're a show-off, is what you are." She stood and carried the dress to the closet to hang it up. "That was very Rhett Butler of you."

"You're lucky I thought to do it like that. Normally, I just throw someone over my shoulder like a sack of potatoes. That's how I've carried my fellow soldiers out of dangerous buildings and situations when they were wounded."

"Good call," she said. "Ladies don't like to be hauled around like potato sacks."

Harley came up to her and placed his hands on her waist. His fingers pressed into the flesh of her hips as he gently stroked the knit fabric of her sweater dress. "I thought that might be the case."

Jade wrapped her arms around his neck. She could feel the dress inching higher on her thighs as he gathered the material in his hands. His gaze never left hers as he reached the hem and lifted it up over her head. As Harley tossed it aside, his blue gaze dipped down to study the treasure he'd uncovered. She'd worn a black strapless bra and a matching thong to try on formals without visible straps or panty lines. Judging by the expression on his face, he approved of the undergarments.

He flattened a hand over her collarbone, then slid his palm down her chest. She wondered if he could feel her heart pounding as he hesitated for a moment, then cupped her left breast through the silky fabric. She reached behind her to unclasp the bra and let it fall to the floor. The movement elicited a groan of appreciation from Harley's lips.

"Beautiful," he whispered as he admired her body.

His palms rose to cover both breasts. The rough feel of his hands against her sensitive nipples teased them into hard peaks, and every graze across their tips sent sparks of pleasure down her spine. She could feel her body grow flush, and heat built between her thighs by the second. She was amazed at how quickly she reacted to Harley. Just a touch, a glance, a wicked smile, and her body was ready for him instantly.

He leaned down to kiss her. This time felt different, though. Maybe it was because this was their first intimate moment since the break-in. Or maybe the last few days had just changed things between them. The urgency was gone, replaced with a gentleness as he sought to savor every moment with her.

Jade leaned into him, molding herself into his embrace. She enjoyed stroking his stubbled jaw, tracing the line of his throat to his collarbone, then on to the row of buttons on his shirt.

His tongue grazed hers, drinking her in even as her fingers undid the last button. She pulled away from his kiss long enough to push the fabric over his shoulders and down to the floor.

Harley took a deep breath and undid his belt. He turned his back to her and walked over to the bed, where he slipped out of the rest of his clothes. He sat on the edge of the bed, eased back to lean against the pillows and watched her from across the room. His appreciative gaze on her body made her feel sexier than she ever had before. She'd always felt too thin, even boyish in shape with no real curves to speak of. But he looked at her like she was the sexiest thing he'd ever seen and she wanted to show off for him.

Jade started by turning her back to him, displaying the curve of her ass in the thin black G-string panties she was wearing. She reached up and pulled the pins from her hair. The twisted bun unraveled, letting the pale blond strands cascade down her bare back and shoulders. She shook it out a little, hearing his sharp intake of breath from the bed.

Then she hooked her thumbs beneath her panties and started easing them over her hips. She did it slowly, bending at the waist as they slid down her legs until she was able to kick them aside. When she turned to face him again, his hands were fisted and his jaw was tight with restraint.

"Come here," was all he said.

Jade moved to the bed, and Harley reached out for her waist and tugged her into his lap. She straddled him, looking into his big blue eyes as he again leaned back against the pillows that lined the padded leather headboard. There were so many unspoken emotions trapped there. If she gazed long enough into their depths, she wondered if she would uncover how he really felt about her. She could easily sense his desire for her. And that he cared for her. But was there more to it than just that? And if there was, would she let her heart have what she wanted this time?

Last time, she'd done what she thought was right and followed her head, not her heart. She'd taken the advice of her well-meaning friends and family, and gone after what she thought she needed in her life. Not what she wanted. Because then, as well as now, Jade wanted Harley. Not just in her bed, but in her life. She wanted to share *his* life. Share his last name. She wanted to share a future with him, even without knowing what that would entail for them.

Because she loved him. If she was honest with

herself, she'd have to admit she loved Harley and always had. She had talked herself out of it, insisted it was youthful infatuation and directed herself onto the "right" path with Lance, but that had never made her a fraction as happy as she was when she was with Harley.

The realization should've made her glad. At last she knew what she wanted in her life. And yet she felt the prickle of tears. Leaning forward, she kissed him and squeezed her eyes shut to keep them from rolling down her cheeks, where Harley could see them.

He wrapped his arms around her body, pulling her tight against his chest and lifting her up just enough for him to slip inside her. She came back down at a tantalizingly slow pace, stopping for a moment to cherish the feel of him. In this moment, they were connected in a way she'd longed for. It wouldn't last forever, though, so she needed to treasure every second they shared like this.

That's how they came together. Rocking back and forth on the bed, riding every high together until her thighs burned, her center throbbed and they couldn't hold out any longer. When she came undone, it wasn't with a cry, but a soft gasp in his ear as she clung to his neck. He followed her, groaning her name in a way that a man wouldn't do unless he felt something for her.

When it was over, Harley gently rolled onto

his side. Scooping Jade into his arms, he tugged her back against his chest and curled protectively around her. "Jade?" he said, in a hushed whisper from behind her.

"Yes?" she replied, her stomach suddenly tightening. He wasn't the kind for pillow talk, so whatever he wanted to say to her right now was important.

"I know you're nervous about meeting the Steeles and what it might mean for you and your future. You always worry about fitting in. But you're amazing," he said. "Don't let anyone ever do or say anything to make you feel otherwise."

It was a sweet thing to say. Something she needed to hear, for sure. But in that moment, it wasn't what she wanted to hear. It had felt like the moment. His chance to say that he wanted more with her. That he cared for her. That he loved her. But instead, she got a lovely compliment and a boost to help her through her nervousness.

She knew then that she couldn't, wouldn't, tell Harley how she felt. Not now, at least. Maybe when the case was over. Right now, it was more important that he focus on what he'd been hired to do. His mind seemed to always be centered there, anyway.

And if he packed up and headed home to DC without a backward glance, she'd be relieved to know she'd kept her mouth shut and hadn't made a fool of herself a second time.

* * *

"You know, if I wasn't seeing it with my own eyes, I wouldn't believe it."

Confused, Harley stopped short in the entryway of Jade's house. The voice he heard didn't make sense in this context. He scanned the room, stopping when he spied Isaiah installing a motion detector in the corner of the kitchen.

"What the hell are you doing here?"

"Installing the equipment you ordered. This is the last of it, actually." Isaiah climbed down from the stepladder and set the drill on the kitchen table. "The cleanup crew is on their way to straighten up the place, too."

Harley shook his head. "That's not what I mean. What are *you* doing here? This isn't your job. You're supposed to be back in DC watching over the office, not putting in cameras and sensors in Charleston."

"It seemed like a rush job, so I came down with the other guys to lend a hand."

Harley stared at his friend in disbelief. "You know better than anyone that you can't lie to me."

Isaiah grinned widely, giving up any pretense about why he was here. "Fine. But do you really think I'd pass up this chance?"

"What chance?"

"To see the great Harley Dalton in love."

"Pish!" Harley said dismissively. "You came down here for nothing, man."

Isaiah crossed his arms over his chest in defiance. "You're not the only one good at picking up when someone is lying. I've known you long enough to tell when you're full of shit. And when you've fallen hard. I wasn't sure I'd ever see the day, but it's here."

Harley didn't want to talk about this right now. Not with Isaiah or anyone else. He didn't know how he felt about Jade, not really. He cared about her. He wanted her badly. He couldn't wait to be back at her side to sweep her into his arms and kiss her again. But that wasn't love. That was just… He didn't know what the hell it was, but he certainly didn't need his best friend telling him how he felt.

"So where's the lucky lady?" Isaiah asked. "I was hoping she might be here with you."

"She's with my mother."

Isaiah's eyebrows went up. "She's met your mother?"

"We dated in high school," Harley snapped. "Of course Jade has met my mother. Besides, I had to take her somewhere when the house was broken into. Mom's house is the safest place I know of in town."

"That's the truth. The Fort Knox of South Carolina." Isaiah looked around the house. "So what's going on with this case, man? I thought it was a baby switcheroo. How'd we get to home invasion and threats?" He gestured toward the spray paint on the living room wall.

Harley followed his gaze and shook his head. He wished he knew. The house was still in shambles after the break-in. He had forced Jade out the door with a suitcase that night and hadn't let her come back. He wouldn't until it was safe. He just wasn't sure when that was going to be. He thought perhaps once the security system was in. Or once the case was solved. Now he wasn't so sure. He felt uneasy when Jade was out of his sight.

But maybe that had more to do with Isaiah's insinuations about love than actual fear for her safety. No matter what, he would feel better when the wacko who broke in was behind bars. He hoped.

"This isn't just a case of a lazy nurse mixing up infants," Harley stated. "This was deliberate. When you called with the information about the Steele family, I was more confident of that fact than ever. Someone deliberately targeted the Steeles' baby. But I don't know why. Nothing ever came of it, best I can tell. Jade's parents went home from the hospital with the daughter they thought was theirs and continued on with their life. There's no damn point to the whole thing. And this..." He lifted his arms to gesture at the mess around them. "There's no reason for this, either. Someone is trying to intimidate her into dropping the case. They've made that clear. But I can't understand what finding out the truth would hurt."

"Unless finding out the truth could uncover the person behind the swap. It's been thirty years, but that doesn't mean they want the cops showing up on their doorstep."

"Maybe. Or maybe the Steele family knows the truth and is desperate to keep it quiet."

"Why?" Isaiah asked. "If they knew they had their own daughter taken from them, why wouldn't they want to know the truth about what happened?"

Harley shrugged. "You said they had politicians and other important people in the family. People like that are different from the rest of us. Maybe they want to avoid scandal at any cost, even if it means raising someone else's child. Or even threatening Jade to keep the story quiet."

"That's ridiculous."

"I know," Harley agreed. He didn't want to think the Steele family was behind the threats, but they certainly weren't cooperating, either. "But I can't explain why else they would ignore my calls. I've phoned both Patricia and Trevor Steele at their home and at his office. I always get housekeepers and assistants who take a message and then no one returns my calls. I have told them who I am and pressed upon them the importance of my call, but have had no response. It seems like they don't want to know the truth."

"What about their daughter, Morgan? Surely she has a vested interest in finding out what happened and meeting her real family."

"I thought the same thing. And when you got me her work information, I called there too and they told me she was out of town on business."

"What about that link I sent you to the charity gig?"

"Yes. That's our saving grace. She's obviously come to Charleston for the event. The Steeles have appearances to keep up, and that means the whole gang will gather tomorrow night at the family compound for their annual charity ball. They hold this fund-raiser and then send teams out with their tools to build housing for the less fortunate."

"They don't sound like arrogant assholes."

They didn't. And that bothered Harley more than anything else. It was hard for him to understand why people who did so much for charity would be so heartless about their own child. It was possible they didn't realize what he was calling about, but he had mentioned Morgan and the hospital. How could they not at least return his call to see what he wanted? To just blow him off seemed out of character, given the facade they presented to the world.

"Are you going to this charity thing, then?"

"Yep. I've got my tuxedo pressed and ready to go. I intend to start up a conversation with Morgan and hopefully get to the bottom of this whole situation."

Isaiah didn't look convinced by his plan. "You're a monster of a man, dude. You've got money, sure, but you don't look like them. You're going to stand out among all those rich, stuffy people. No one is going to think you're a guest. At best, they'll think you're undercover security. You're way too conspicuous."

"That's why I'm taking a date."

"You're not taking Jade, are you?" Isaiah asked, a wary expression in his eyes.

"She insisted, and she was right. She said the same thing you did. I need a date to fit in or I won't make it past the front door, ticket or not."

"A date, yes. But Jade? There's a lot of personal crap involved there. You don't think that taking her is a bad idea? This is potentially her family she's meeting for the first time. You're there to get information. She's there to see the life she's missed out on. What if your objectives are at cross-purposes? She could panic and blow your cover. She could say or do something to get you thrown out before you can do what you went to accomplish. If it comes down to Jade or the job, what will you choose?"

"It's just a bunch of rich people mingling and writing checks so they can feel better about themselves. I can't imagine it being so dire that it would come down to me choosing between my case and Jade."

Isaiah crossed his arms over his chest and sighed. "Then you need to imagine harder."

Eleven

Whoa. *Money.*

The Steele mansion was ridiculous. It was exactly what Jade would've pictured: a typical two-story plantation home, with a long driveway that led up to it, lined by oaks dripping with Spanish moss. It was white, with massive columns that reached for the sky and huge windows flanked by black shutters. There was a line of cars out front and a crowd of people walking up the stairs to the open entrance. There were valets in dark green suits greeting the guests and taking their cars to a grass lot around the side of the property.

When they pulled up, Jade found her heart pounding so hard in her chest she could barely breathe.

This was it. Harley was fairly certain that her real parents were Trevor and Patricia Steele. Pictures she'd seen on the internet had only confirmed his suspicions. Jade was no doubt a younger version of Patricia.

In a few moments, she would walk through the front door of their home and lay eyes on them in person for the very first time. She would probably be able to pick them out of a crowd. But what would they think when they saw her? She didn't know.

It was her idea to come tonight. She had sworn to Harley that she could keep her cool. Yet in the moment, she found she couldn't make herself reach for the handle to open the passenger door. It wasn't until the valet did so with a smile and offered to help her out that she started to move. Jade gathered up her small beaded clutch and stepped out of the Jaguar to face her future.

Harley came around the front of the car and took her arm. "Are you okay?" he asked.

"Why?"

"You seem a little tense."

She tried to smile and dismiss both their worries. "I'm just nervous. I'll be fine." She took a deep breath. "So, do we have a plan of action for tonight?"

"Observe. Try to talk to the family, especially Morgan, if we can. That's it. I don't intend to make a scene. I really just want to make the connection without their staff in the way. I'm certain once they realize the seriousness of the situation, they will fully cooperate."

At the top of the stairs, they stepped into the grand foyer, where they turned in their tickets and were greeted by servers with flutes of champagne. They each accepted a glass and continued toward the sound of music and laughter coming from the far side of the house.

"Nice," Jade said, after she took a sip of the champagne. It was dry, but had a sweet finish and enough bubbles to tickle her nose. "I wasn't expecting it to be so good. I could get used to this."

"It should be nice. Tickets to the party were ten thousand dollars a couple, and I'm not even sure they're serving a meal."

Jade came to a sudden stop and turned to look at Harley. There were easily a couple hundred people at this event so far. "Are you serious?"

He nodded. "They're raising money for charity and most of these people have the cash to burn and tax deductions to seek out. You're not going to build houses for the poor charging twenty bucks a head."

She nervously took another sip of her champagne and hoped the alcohol would calm her nerves. This was the life she very well could've been born to. It was a surreal thought. But not so surreal as the sight of the ballroom when they stepped through the wide French doors.

The room was huge, with gold and crystal chandeliers hanging overhead and thick velvet drapes framing each picture window. An orchestra was in the corner playing to the crowd on the dance floor, which was surrounded by dozens of round tables draped in gray and red fabric and topped with tall floral arrangements of bright red roses. Those were the Steele Company colors, of course. The sight was almost as overwhelming as the sound of music and hundreds of voices coming at them like a wave.

"Are you ready?" Harley asked.

Jade threw back the last of her champagne and set the flute on the tray of a passing server. "As ready as I'll ever be."

Harley smiled and led her through the crowds of people to one of the tables that had empty seats. He left Jade for a moment to go to the bar and get more drinks for them. When he returned, he sat beside her for a moment, seeming to want to give her time to acclimate.

"What now?" she asked.

He scanned the room thoughtfully. To their right was a big buffet display with hot and cold appetizers and a large bar. On the other side was the dance floor, where quite a few people had gathered. "May I have this dance?" he asked.

"I'm not a very good dancer," she admitted.

"Neither am I. I just want us mingling. It'll make it easier to track down the family." Harley pushed up from his seat and offered Jade his hand. She accepted it and he led her through the maze of tables. They found a spot near the center of the dancefloor and blended in with the rest of the crowd. The music was slow and steady, allowing Harley to take Jade in his arms and rock back and forth in an easy rhythm.

Jade finally relaxed, with his hand resting warm and secure on her lower back. Things seemed easier when he touched her, somehow. It made her wonder how she was going to deal with what was to come without him.

"Have I mentioned how beautiful you look tonight?"

She gazed up at him and smiled. "Almost enough times to make me believe it."

"I know this probably isn't the right time to say this," he said, "but I need to get it off my chest. The music and the champagne are making me brave."

Jade stiffened in his arms. "What is it?"

"I should've fought for you," he said. "Back then. I'm sorry I didn't. I know you always feel like you aren't good enough, and I understand what it's like because I've never felt like I was good enough for you, either. That's why I didn't fight. I wanted to. I wanted to drive to Clemson, knock on your dormitory door and kiss you until you couldn't even remember Lance's name. But I thought you'd be better off without me."

She didn't know what to say. What would she

have done if he'd followed his heart? How would their lives be now?

"I'm not sure what's going to happen tonight. Or next week. I'm not sure about a lot of things. But I know I don't want to make the same mistake with you twice. Jade, I..."

The song that was playing ended. That's when the band leader called the Steele family to the stage and they started to make their way to the front of the ballroom.

This was the moment Jade had been waiting for, and yet she wished she could put the whole party on pause to hear what he wanted to tell her. He looked reluctantly at the gathering and gave her a sad smile. "To be continued," he said.

Jade squeezed her eyes shut in frustration for a moment, then tried to focus on what was going on with the group gathering onstage. They were easily some of the most beautiful people she had ever seen in person. It was as though they'd all walked off the cover of a magazine. She easily recognized Trevor and Patricia from their photo. They were standing together, sharing a quiet moment of conversation. Trevor was tall and lean with graying, honey-gold hair and dark eyes. Patricia had Jade's same white-blond hair and high cheekbones. She was very slender, like Jade, and carried herself with unmistakable poise.

Their children were gathered near them. Three

sons, all handsome, all spitting images of their father. It looked as though two of them might even be identical twins, although Jade couldn't be sure. Perhaps it was just their flawless tuxedos and bright smiles that made them appear so alike. Then she turned her gaze toward the woman one of the sons was speaking to, and that's when Jade realized it was none other than Morgan Steele.

Jade froze in place, taking in every feature of the dark beauty. Morgan was a marked contrast to the rest of her family, with her thick, almost black hair and green eyes. In that moment, she looked so much like Jade's mother that Jade felt a punch of jealousy to her stomach. She had always wanted to fit in, to look like the rest of her family. Morgan fit in perfectly and she didn't even know it.

And yet she fit in with the Steele family, as well. She had a different look to her, but she also had their regal carriage, their elegance and their confidence. Morgan wore her emerald gown and sparking jewelry as if they were made just for her. She would fit in anywhere she chose to and people would flock to her.

Then there was Jade. She'd felt so pretty in her dress tonight. And in an instant she might as well have worn a T-shirt and jeans to the party.

She'd come here tonight in the hopes of finding out where she belonged. In her mind, she'd thought that somehow seeing her biological family would make the pieces click together and suddenly her life would make sense. But it didn't. In that moment, she wanted nothing more than to sit around the worn kitchen table at her parents' house and play a board game with them and her brother. They had never made her feel like she was an outsider in the family. Jade was the only one who seemed to notice the differences.

They'd never said it, but it had to have hurt them to have Jade pursue her real family so doggedly. It wasn't as though they hadn't been the best parents a girl could ask for. They had been. She wouldn't trade them for the world, and she hoped they knew that.

She wanted to go and tell them that right now. To walk away from all this before she couldn't turn back.

The longer she stood watching the family mingle, the more she realized this wasn't what she wanted. This was a mistake. Someone didn't want the truth to come out, and now she wasn't so certain that she wanted the truth to come out, either. Maybe it was better to leave well enough alone.

"I'd like to welcome everyone," Trevor Steele said as he stepped forward with the microphone in his hand. "My name is Trevor Steele and I'm the current CEO of Steele Tools. This is my beautiful family." He gestured toward the others on the stage, beaming with pride as the crowd applauded. "We are all so thrilled to have you here with us tonight to make a difference for those in need. I'd like to invite my incredibly talented daughter, Morgan, the head of our community outreach program, to step up to the microphone to tell you all a little about why we've gathered here tonight and what you can do to help."

Morgan moved gracefully across the stage, accepting a kiss on the cheek from her doting father as she took the microphone. "Write a big check," she said with a grin, and the crowd laughed.

Everyone seemed to be having a good time tonight. They got to dress up, mingle with their peers and feel like they were giving back and doing something good. The room was charged with positive energy. And Jade had never wanted to get out of a place more in her life.

"Harley, I've changed my mind. I want to go home."

He stiffened, turning to her with a stunned expression on his face. "You what?" he whispered, trying not to draw attention to them while Morgan spoke onstage.

"I want to go home. I think this whole thing was a mistake. I—I don't know if this is the right thing to do."

Damn it. He knew bringing Jade was a potentially bad idea, but he couldn't say no to her. She was his weakness and now she would potentially ruin his chance to get to the Steele family. He'd barely laid eyes on them, and had come nowhere close to actually speaking to any of the Steeles. "You're just nervous," he soothed. Harley reached for her elbow and led her off the dance floor.

Once they were clear of most of the crowd listening to the speeches, he stopped and turned to her. "It's totally understandable to be anxious about something like this. This is a big deal. I won't even pretend to know how big it is for you. But running away isn't going to change the truth, Jade."

She pulled away from his hold and hugged her own waist apprehensively. "It may not change the truth, but I'm starting to think it's better this way. Things worked out the way they should've. The family seems so happy. I don't want to mess that up for them. Or hurt my own parents more than I already have. I'll call the hospital myself and tell them I'm dropping my claim against them."

"It's too late for that. Come on, Jade, think about the people who broke into your home. They were trying to stop you from finding out the truth. If you give up now, they win."

"It doesn't matter. It's been thirty years. This isn't my life and it never will be. I'd rather let it lie."

Harley squeezed his eyes shut. He wanted to shake some sense into her, although he wouldn't dare. He had to find a way to reason with her. There was no way to stop the train once it left the station. Whether she wanted it to, whether he dropped the investigation… The hospital administrators knew there was an issue now and they would get to the bottom of it.

He reached out and gripped her upper arm, feeling she might run from the ball like Cinderella if he didn't. "I can't let it lie, Jade. This is my job. A job I was hired for because of you. And I was hired to find out the truth. I'm going to do that whether you want me to anymore or not."

A flash of pain danced across Jade's pale face before she jerked herself from his grip. Her dark eyes grew glassy as she slowly shook her head in disbelief and heartache.

"Jade…" He reached out again.

"No. Don't," she argued, stepping out of his reach. "You have your priorities and I have mine. I thought I might rank higher on your list, but that was foolish of me. I wasn't Lance's priority, either. He was more interested in getting high and you're more interested in the thrill of the chase."

The crowd applauded loudly and the orchestra started playing again. They both turned to see the Steeles step down from the stage and return to mingling with their guests and donors. If Harley was going to talk to Morgan, he needed to do it soon. If he could just convince Jade to give him ten minutes… Just ten minutes could make all the difference in the world.

He turned back to her with pleading eyes. "That's not true."

She shook her head more adamantly. "We'll see about that. Go on, go be the badass who saves the day. But I'm going home, Harley. Home to my own house. I'll ask one of the valets to call a cab to pick me up." Jade spun on her heel, a blur of crimson beading, and then made a beeline for the ballroom entrance.

Harley reached out for her, about to chase her down and beg for her to wait a little bit longer. That's when he saw it. His moment. His chance.

Out of the corner of his eyes, he spied Patricia Steele setting her empty champagne flute on a nearby table. If he could pick up the glass before a waiter got to it, he could get a DNA sample and confirm his suspicions even if the family wouldn't cooperate. They'd answer the phone when the hospital's attorneys called, he was pretty sure.

He tore his gaze away from the glass for a moment to see Jade slip out of the ballroom and toward the front of the house. If he moved fast enough, he could get the glass and reach Jade before she could arrange a ride back to her house. She wouldn't be happy with him for grabbing the glass after she'd asked him to stop investigating and leave the party, but that was a risk he was willing to take. An opportunity didn't come wrapped in a bow like this very often.

Darting through the crowds of milling people, he reached the table and snatched up the flute. Holding it as though it were his own, he slipped away and headed toward the door. He looked around to make sure no one was watching, then tucked it in his coat's inner breast pocket. It would go in an evidence bag the first chance he got without a crowd of witnesses.

But first, to catch up with Jade.

This evening was not going at all the way he'd hoped. It was supposed to be a night of breakthroughs. They were supposed to connect with her family and usher in that happy reunion. He had even been on the verge of telling her how he felt about her when they were out on the dance floor.

If the speeches had come even a minute later, the words that had been lingering on the tip of his tongue would've gotten out. He would have told Jade that he loved her. And maybe then, when the fear got to her, she would've known that he was doing this for her. Not in spite of her.

Harley made his way through the house. He paused at the registration desk near the entrance. "Did a woman in a red dress come by here just now?" he asked. If she'd hidden in the restroom instead of going outside, they wouldn't have seen her.

There were two women at the table and they

both nodded. "She went out about a minute ago. She seemed upset," the older lady said with a look of disapproval.

He went past them and down the front stairs to the circular driveway, where the valets were mostly sitting idle. Jade was nowhere to be found. "Which way did the woman in red go?" he asked.

The group of men all pointed to the far side of the house. Perhaps she'd gone that way trying to get better cell phone reception.

Harley jogged to the end of the building, expecting to see her there calling for a ride. And she was. But before he could say anything, a white van pulled to a stop in front of her. The door flew open and in a blur of red, Jade was pulled inside by two men in dark clothes. The door slammed shut and the van's tires squealed loudly as it took off from the driveway and roared down the narrow lane away from the house.

Harley took off on foot after it, shouting Jade's name, as though he had a chance in hell of catching it. But as the taillights disappeared into the distance, he came to a stop. His lungs burned in his chest even as his heart ached just as fiercely. He'd promised Jade he would keep her safe. He'd promised he would solve the case quickly so she wouldn't have to live in fear of the threats any longer.

Turning on his heel, he ran back to the house, yelling for the valets to call the police and report the abduction. He couldn't take back what had just happened, but he could redeem himself in her eyes and his own by doing everything he could to bring her home safely.

She'd thought she was safe with him. He'd taken his eye off her for only a moment. A big mistake, especially after she'd asked him to leave with her.

But Jade was right. He'd chosen the job and the glory over her. He just hoped he wouldn't regret that decision for the rest of his life.

Twelve

Jade rolled around the back of the van and hit her head against the metal wall with a dull thud. At least she thought it was the wall. It was hard to tell with the blindfold over her eyes. She wasn't thinking too clearly anyway. Her head was already throbbing from the strong whiff of chloroform they'd used to disable her. They hadn't given her enough of a dose to knock her out cold—that took a few minutes and some dedication—but it did its job in disorienting her enough that they could drag her into their vehicle. Now she was dizzy, with a pounding head and a bad attitude.

"Ow!" She groaned loudly as she felt the knot rise up on her forehead and a warm trickle run down the side of her face. It was probably blood. And with her hands tied together, she was unable to stop the bumping and brace herself as the van sped around corners. She was like a rag doll back here, feeling the beading of her dress catch and snag as she slid across the unfinished floor.

Abduction aside, the thought of the beautiful gown Harley had bought her being ruined brought angry tears to her eyes.

"Slow down or we're gonna get caught," one man hissed, presumably at the driver. His voice was gravelly, like he'd smoked three packs a day for thirty years.

"If I slow down, we *will* get caught. We've got to get the hell away from the Steele mansion first. That guy is crazy enough to follow us."

"I don't see his Jaguar behind us. I think we're safe."

"You're an idiot," the second man said. His voice was deeper, but smooth as silk. "There's no such thing as safe until we've got the money in hand, the woman is back with her rich family and we're chilling on a beach in Puerto Vallarta. Then and only then will I take the first deep breath I've taken in thirty years."

Jade tried to ease back until she was leaning against the side of the van for some stability. She didn't make a peep, not wanting to interrupt her captors' conversation. She intended to memorize every word so when she got out of this mess, she could turn all of it over to Harley and the police.

Provided she actually got out of this. She didn't know what these guys wanted with her, but it couldn't be good. One of them had mentioned money, so maybe this was just about ransom. That seemed a stupid choice. Her family didn't have any money. At least, not the family who had raised her. Maybe these two knew even more about Jade than she did.

"Here's the turn," the man with the gravelly voice said.

"I know where the damn turn is. I don't need you to tell me how to drive. I've got this under control." The van slowed and went over a bump. "I learned my lesson after the last time, when your sister screwed us both."

"Screwed *us*? She's the one who died, not you."

"Yeah, well, if she was feeling so guilty that she was thinking about doing something like that, she should've turned over some crucial information first. Like which damn baby was which. We've sat on our hands for three decades because of her stupid conscience and I'm not taking that risk a second time. I want my money and I want this done."

"Do you think they'll pay for her? They don't even know who she is."

"She's their blood. They'll pay. And if not, well, maybe we go after the big guy. Did you see how long he ran after us? Like he was gonna catch the van. That dope is in love. I'm willing to bet he'll shell out whatever we ask."

Jade's breath caught in her throat. They had to be talking about Harley. She hadn't seen him outside. Had he followed her out in time to see the men take her? She hoped so. He'd chased after her. She didn't know if she could take these thug's word for it, but they seemed to think Harley was in love with her. She couldn't believe it.

They'd better hope they were wrong. If he did love her, these men better pray the cops found them first.

She heard the sound of a metal garage door going up as the van came to a stop. The vehicle inched forward and finally the engine shut off. The metal door started creaking again, likely closing this time, trapping her in whatever garage or warehouse they'd chosen to take cover from the cops.

They'd probably be headed to the back of the van to deal with her soon. Jade took a deep breath and hoped she had the strength to get through this. To see Harley and her parents again. Her real parents. The Steeles might be lovely people, but the faces she wanted to see belonged to Arthur and Carolyn Nolan.

"All right, we're here," the driver said. "It's time to make the call."

Harley marched back into the ballroom, and casting aside any pretense of being a normal guest or donor, went straight up to Trevor and Patricia Steele. "Are you behind this?" he asked, unable to keep the anger from his voice.

The couple turned to him with wide, surprised eyes. They didn't look as though people took that tone with them very often. "Are we behind what, sir?" Trevor asked, with a sharp edge to his voice.

"Someone just abducted Jade from your driveway. If you're behind this, tell me now."

"Abducted?" Patricia said, bringing a hand to her chest in dismay. "Jade who?"

"Your daughter, Jade. The one I've been trying to call you about for the last week."

They looked genuinely confused by the entire conversation. As much as he wanted to leap ahead, it seemed as though he'd have to go backward. "My name is Harley Dalton, with Dalton Security. I've been calling you both repeatedly this week about a case at St. Francis Hospital. Did you not get any of my messages?"

"No," Trevor said, looking mildly irritated, albeit not with Harley. "Although the week leading up to the gala is usually so hectic. My staff might've been remiss in passing your messages along. They tend to filter out what they deem unnecessary when we're so busy. We get a lot of calls. You're working for St. Francis Hospital, you say?"

"Yes, where your wife gave birth to a daughter during Hurricane Hugo in 1989."

"Our daughter, Morgan, is right over there." Patricia gestured to her. "I don't understand what's going on."

Harley didn't want to be the one to say this, but the sooner they all got on the same page the better. "That is not your biological child. Two of the infants in the nursery were switched during the storm. Your daughter was raised by the Nolan family, who recently uncovered the mix-up during DNA testing. The woman you know as your daughter, Morgan, is actually their daughter, Jade."

Harley watched Trevor Steele's face blanch for a moment as he absorbed the news. Before he could gauge any more of their reactions, a man ran up to the two of them with a wild-eyed expression on his face. "Mr. Steele, the police are here. They said they got a call about an abduction."

Harley was about to step in, but Trevor collected himself and beat him to it. The CEO instantly began barking orders at everyone around him. "See them into the library, please. We will be there momentarily." He turned to his wife. "Patricia, go get Morgan and meet us in the library. I'll have the boys clear out the room. The party is over."

Harley breathed a sigh of relief that the family was taking this seriously. He watched as Patricia escorted a confused-looking Morgan out of the ballroom, while her father went in search of his sons to handle the other guests. Trevor appeared at Harley's side a moment later. "I'm sorry that we didn't get in touch with you sooner, Mr. Dalton. I will be having words with my staff once this is cleared up. Let's head over to the library. A flood of people are about to come through here once my oldest makes the announcement."

The Steeles were cool and collected in the face of drama, something that both confused and concerned Harley. It wasn't until they reached the library and sat down with the detectives that he understood why.

"This isn't our first kidnapping, Mr. Dalton, so I'm sorry if we seem unaffected by this. We've learned the hard way to save emotions for later, once what needs to be done is done."

Harley made his statement to the police, letting the family listen in anxiously as he recounted the threats, the break-in and finally Jade's abduction from the property. She and the Steeles were related; they had to be. And if the Steele family wasn't trying to keep Jade quiet, he had no leads on who the kidnappers could be.

The police were sending a crew to the house to set up a surveillance team in case the kidnappers called in a ransom request. In the meantime, every cop in the city would be looking for a white van with South Carolina plates that started with the number 7.

"This is our fault," Patricia said, once the police stepped out and left them alone together in the library.

She'd been sitting on the couch, holding a dumbfounded Morgan against her side for the last hour. Harley couldn't begin to imagine how the young woman was processing everything under circumstances like this. "It's happening again, just like with Tommy."

Trevor came around the couch and placed his hand on his wife's shoulder. "We got Tom back safe and sound, and the same will happen here. We will get Jade back, and then we will find out what happened at the hospital and why."

"So someone switched babies, then thirty years later, they kidnapped the one who's really our sister?" one of the twins asked. It was either Finn or Sawyer, Harley wasn't sure. The young man stood by the window looking confused.

"Morgan is your sister," Trevor insisted, pointing to the woman on the couch. "In every way that is important. But yes, if this man is correct, your biological sister, Jade, was taken because she was trying to find her family and someone didn't want that to happen."

Morgan stood up from the couch, her eyes red, but tearless. "I'm going upstairs," she said. She rushed from the room.

"Let her go, Patricia," Trevor said. "This is a lot for her to take in. What's important for her to know—and for all of us to impress upon her—is that she is no less a member of this family because of what happened."

Harley was pleased to hear them say that. He was equally hopeful that they would welcome Jade with that same attitude. She deserved that much, especially after he'd basically forced her into going through with it all tonight. What if he'd just taken her home instead of arguing with her? They'd be in bed, holding each other, instead of him waiting anxiously for a phone call or news from the police about Jade's whereabouts.

"I wish they would just call already," Patricia said. "The waiting is the worst part."

As though the kidnappers had heard her plea, a phone started to ring. They all expected it to be the Steeles' home phone, where the police had the lines tapped, but it was Harley's cell phone.

He didn't recognize the number, but he answered, putting it on speakerphone so everyone could listen in. "Hello?"

"Ten million dollars," a raspy male voice said. "Small, unmarked bills. Fill a black tote bag with the money and leave it in locker 17 at the bus station downtown by ten tomorrow morning. If you follow my instructions and we're able to pick up the money without police interference, I will text you the location of the woman. If the cops are waiting for us, or we get intercepted in any way, you'll never see her again."

"I want to talk to Jade," Harley insisted, but the man just laughed and hung up. As the line went dead, he felt a sense of hope rise up to battle the ache of dread in his stomach. They just wanted money. He had plenty of that. He'd happily comply with their instructions to get Jade back safely. He just had to hope that the kidnappers played by their own rules.

"Ten million is a lot to get our hands on in less than twelve hours," Trevor said.

"I know," Harley said. He'd learned early that to make money he had to keep his cash tied up in things that would continue to earn for him. Untangling that was not a quick job. "I'll have to think of something. I can easily get my hands on maybe a third of that."

"How much do we have in the safe, darling?" Patricia asked her husband.

"Four, I think. Maybe four and a half. We could get more wired over without a problem. It's morning in Switzerland, isn't it?" Trevor walked over to where Harley was standing and patted him on the back. "Between the two of us, we'll get Jade back safely. Never fear, she's one of us now. And in this family, we live by the strict motto of No Steele Left Behind."

Jade heard a noise and shot to attention on the cold steel wall she was slumped against. She wished she could pull off her blindfold and see what was happening, but it was impossible with the zip ties on her wrists and ankles.

She'd been alone for a while, but she wasn't sure how long. She'd heard the men talk about going to get the money and then they left in the van. They didn't say much to her while they kept her captive, but they left her with parting words that chilled her to the core… The next thing she saw would either be her rescuers if all went well, or the two of them before they put a bullet in her head.

If someone was here, wherever she was, she was about to find out which it would be.

"Jade!"

"Harley? Harley!" Jade heard his heavy footsteps pounding across concrete toward her. She breathed a sigh of relief at the sound of his voice and felt the tears start rolling down her cheeks. She hadn't allowed herself to panic; she didn't have that luxury. But now all her emotions were pouring out of her at once.

She felt someone drop to the ground beside her and rip off her blindfold. Her eyes struggled to adjust to the light after hours in total darkness, but she could make out Harley crouched beside her. He made quick work of the ties on her ankles and wrists, allowing the blood to flow into her extremities again.

"Oh my God, baby, I'm so glad you're okay. I'm so sorry. I never should've let you out of my sight." Harley clutched her to his chest and she happily curled up against him.

She'd spent a long night with her thoughts, reliving what had happened before and after the abduction. She knew she'd overreacted. And in this dire situation, her dangerous bad boy was the only man qualified for the job. He was up to the task, and for that, she would be eternally grateful.

"It wasn't your fault," she croaked with a hoarse, dry throat. "You saved me."

"Of course I saved you." He sat back and cupped her face in his hands. "I love you, Jade. More than you can ever imagine. I would do anything to bring you home to me."

He loved her? Jade was overwhelmed by everything going on, but she couldn't let that detail pass by unnoticed. "Did you say you loved me?" she asked.

Harley smiled. "I did. I love you, Jade Nolan. Very much. I only wish I'd gotten to tell you before all this happened. For a while last night, I thought I might not get the chance."

Jade brought her hand to his cheek. It was very stubbly, as he probably hadn't shaved or showered. He was still wearing his tuxedo, minus the bow tie. His eyes were lined with worry and he looked as exhausted as she felt. And yet he was the most beautiful thing she'd ever seen. "I love you, too, Harley."

He leaned in and pressed his lips to hers. The kiss was loaded with emotions they'd both held in. Now it all poured out at once. Love, relief, need, happiness. She pulled away from his kiss only when she had to cough. She'd been hacking most of the morning.

"I'm sorry. My throat is so dry. I haven't had anything to drink since the champagne at the party."

"I can fix that." Harley lifted a phone to his ear. "She's here. Yes, she's safe. Bring the blanket and the water."

As Jade looked up, she noticed there was a virtual crowd of people rushing over to her. She recognized the silhouettes of her parents immediately. Arthur and Carolyn swooped in, practically nudging Harley aside to hold their daughter. She had never been happier to see her family.

"Are you okay, honey?" Carolyn asked. She brushed the hair from Jade's eyes and studied the bump on her head. "You're bleeding."

"I'm fine, Mama. I'm just happy to see you."

Arthur squeezed her shoulder and smiled. "There's some other people here that are happy to see you, too." He stood and stepped aside to reveal another couple hovering nearby.

It was Trevor and Patricia Steele. They were standing awkwardly at a distance, obviously wanting to help somehow, but not wanting to intrude on her moment with Harley and her parents.

Patricia stepped forward at last, crouching down to hand Jade a bottle of water they'd brought with them. "Here you go, dear. I'm so glad you're safe. We were worried sick all night."

Those were words she wasn't expecting. A lot must have happened while she was tied up in this warehouse. "Really?"

Harley smiled and rubbed her back encouragingly. "They know everything. They even helped pay the ransom."

Trevor came up beside his wife and got down onto one knee. "No Steele Left Behind," he said with a smile. He studied her face for a moment, then shook his head in amazement. "You look almost exactly like your mother did at that age. It's uncanny."

He reached out and put a comforting hand on her shoulder. "We've got a lot to talk about, little girl, but let's get you out of here first. We have plenty of time to catch up."

Harley helped her up off the concrete floor and wrapped her in a blanket Trevor brought in with them. Jade was content to disappear into the cocoon of soft wool as they walked slowly out of the warehouse to awaiting cars. The Steeles waved to her before they piled into a black Escalade with a uniformed driver. Beside it was her father's minivan and the Jaguar, parked haphazardly as though Harley had rushed in to find her.

"Harley has to take you to the police station to get your statement and let you get checked out,"

Carolyn said. “You call us later and let us know you’re okay.”

“Yes, Mama.” Carolyn kissed her on the cheek, and then let Arthur guide her over to the van.

As they pulled away, Harley helped Jade into his car, then came around his side to sit down beside her. Instead of starting the engine, he reached for her hand and held it tightly in his. “Before we go to the station, there’s something I need to say. Jade… I would’ve done anything to get you back.”

“Including paying my captors ten million dollars?” she asked. The sum seemed ridiculous, but her kidnappers were aiming high.

“In a heartbeat. I’d pay it again if I had to.”

Jade looked into his blue eyes, which were glassy with tears, and felt her chest tighten with emotion. “Don’t say that loud enough for those guys to hear you or they might try this again. Unless they’ve been…*caught*?” she asked.

Harley shook his head. “Unfortunately, no. The police were watching the bus station, but had to wait to move in until after those thugs texted your location to me. By then they were long gone, and the cops lost them in the maze of streets downtown. But we’ll find them. You can count on it.”

“Another exciting job for you to take on,” Jade said with a rueful smile.

“I think I’m going to leave most of that to the police. The last twelve hours have provided enough excitement to last me a lifetime," Harley said. "The only rush I need is the feeling of you in my arms and the flutter of nerves in my stomach when I see you smile at me from across the room. I'd happily sit behind my desk and live a safe and secure life with you until I draw my last breath. Which hopefully will be well into my eighties or nineties."

"You really mean that?"

"I sure do. Let me prove it."

Harley reached across her to the glove compartment of the car and pulled out a small box that was instantly recognizable. He opened it and offered it to her, showcasing the sparking ring in its bed of navy velvet. It was beautiful. The center was a large princess-cut diamond set in platinum, and in the band were alternating round diamonds and dark blue sapphires. "As a navy vet, I thought perhaps some sapphires were appropriate."

"When did you have time to get an engagement ring?" she asked. After everything that had happened, it was the last thing she'd expected.

"Before the party," he said. "It was in my coat pocket the whole time. I was going to give it to you after we left the gala, but that didn't really work out."

She just stared at the ring, anxious to reach out and slip it on her finger, yet waiting on him to ask her the all-important question first.

"Jade Nolan…last night was the worst night of my life. I wanted to marry you before all this happened, but now I truly can't imagine a day of my life without you. We've already lost over a decade and I don't want to lose a minute more. Will you do me the honor of being my wife?"

Jade smiled and leaned in to give him a kiss. There was no question this time that she would follow her heart. "Yes," she whispered against his lips. "A million times, yes."

Epilogue

Jade never thought she'd see the moment that both sets of her parents would be sitting together, enjoying a warm spring day on the top deck of the Steeles' luxury yacht, the *License to Drill.* But here they were, along with Harley, all her brothers and Morgan, to celebrate their engagement.

After weeks of working through the details, taking DNA tests and verifying the results to everyone's satisfaction, the families had come together in the first of many events. It was a bittersweet moment for Jade, to realize she would now be sharing her parents with Morgan, but seeing the tears in her mother Carolyn's eyes was worth it.

The two families were so different, and yet they

were united in their desire to share Morgan and Jade, and build a relationship together. After all, they would always be tied together by the strange twist of fate that swapped their babies that day.

Jade sipped her mimosa and watched everyone with a smile on her face. Her old brother, Dean, and her new brother Finn, were deep-sea fishing. Her mothers were sharing stories about what the girls were like as babies. Her fathers were discussing the different virtues of Scotch while they stood at the bar. It had turned out better than she ever expected it to.

There were still loose ends, but she knew those would be resolved in time. Her kidnappers would be found, and maybe they would be able to find out if the thugs were involved in the original switch. They still didn't know for sure, although the conversation Jade had overheard in the van certainly made it sound like the two crimes were connected. She had relayed all the information she could remember, but knew there were details she'd forgotten in all the chaos. Despite his initial disinterest, Harley was still working that angle of the case, this time with the Steeles fully cooperating and partially funding the investigation.

It was hard to think about all that, though. It was much more pleasant to focus on her upcoming wedding to Harley, and her newly expanding family.

"I had the sweetest nurse at St. Francis," she

heard her mother Carolyn say. "I've been trying to remember her name since all this started and it's been making me crazy. Did you have her? She was a redhead. Big smile. Very chatty."

"I think I do remember her," Patricia said. "I wasn't having the greatest labor and she kept talking. I wanted more than anything for her to shut up and go away. I want to say it was something like Noreen? Tracy? Nadine?"

"Nancy?" Harley interjected.

"That's it!" both women said together.

"Nancy. Thank you," Carolyn said. "That's been driving me mad."

The conversation continued, but Harley made his way across the deck to where Jade was sitting. "How did you know the name?" she asked.

"I have the personnel files from the hospital. There was a nurse named Nancy working that day. A nurse who just so happened to kill herself less than a week after you and Morgan were swapped."

Jade's sharp intake of breath was barely audible over the ocean breeze and the sound of the music playing through the deck speakers. "Do you think she was involved?"

"It had to be an inside job."

"I wish I remembered more from the night of the kidnapping. I feel like they said something important, but the whole night has blurred together.

Maybe if we find more information, it will jog my memory."

"Maybe so. Let's see what we can find."

Harley didn't hesitate to pick up his phone and dial Isaiah. While it rang, he leaned in and kissed Jade hard enough to make her blush.

"Hey," he said into the phone, as he pulled away and gave her a wink that promised more, and soon. "I need you to find out everything you can about a former St. Francis labor and delivery nurse named Nancy."

* * * * *

Why were Jade and Morgan switched at birth?
How will Morgan adjust to the surprise of her life?

If you loved Jade and Harley, you're not going to want to miss Morgan's story,
From Riches to Redemption,
by Andrea Laurence.

Available August 2019 wherever Harlequin Desire books are sold.

COMING NEXT MONTH FROM

Available July 1, 2019

#2671 MARRIED IN NAME ONLY

Texas Cattleman's Club: Houston • by Jules Bennett

Facing an explosive revelation about her real father, Paisley Morgan has no one to turn to except her ex, wealthy investigator Lucas Ford. Lucas has one condition for doing business with the woman who unceremoniously dumped him, though—a marriage of convenience to settle the score!

#2672 RED HOT RANCHER

by Maureen Child

Five years ago, Emma Williams left home for dreams of Hollywood—right before rancher Caden Hale could propose. Now she's back, older and wiser—and with a baby! Will the newly wealthy cowboy want a rematch?

#2673 SEDUCED BY SECOND CHANCES

Dynasties: Secrets of the A-List • by Reese Ryan

Singer-songwriter Jessica Humphrey is on the brink of fame when a performance brings her face-to-face with the one man she's always desired but could never have—her sister's ex, Gideon Johns. Will their unstoppable passion be her downfall? Or can she have it all?

#2674 ONE NIGHT, WHITE LIES

The Bachelor Pact • by Jessica Lemmon

When Reid Singleton buys the beautiful stranger a drink, he doesn't realize she's actually his best friend's little sister, Drew Fleming—until after he sleeps with her! Will their fledgling relationship survive...as even bigger family secrets threaten to derail everything?

#2675 A CINDERELLA SEDUCTION

The Eden Empire • by Karen Booth

Newly minted heiress Emma Stewart is desperate to be part of the powerful family she never knew. But when she realizes her very own Prince Charming comes from a rival family set on taking hers down, the stakes of seduction couldn't get higher...

#2676 A TANGLED ENGAGEMENT

Takeover Tycoons • by Tessa Radley

Hard-driving fashion executives Jay Black and Georgia Kinnear often butt heads. But Jay won't just stand by and let her controlling father marry her off to another man—especially when Jay has his own plan to make her his fake fiancée!

YOU CAN FIND MORE INFORMATION ON UPCOMING HARLEQUIN® TITLES, FREE EXCERPTS AND MORE AT WWW.HARLEQUIN.COM.

HDCNM0619

When Reid Singleton buys the beautiful stranger a drink, he doesn't realize she's actually his best friend's little sister, Drew Fleming—until after he sleeps with her! Will their fledgling relationship survive...as even bigger family secrets threaten to derail everything?

Read on for a sneak peek at
One Night, White Lies
by Jessica Lemmon!

London-born Reid Singleton didn't know a damn thing about women's shoes. So when he became transfixed by a pair on the dance floor, fashion wasn't his dominating thought.

They were pink, but somehow also metallic, with long Grecian-style straps crisscrossing delicate, gorgeous ankles. He curled his scotch to his chest and backed into the shadows, content to watch the woman who owned those ankles for a bit.

From those pinkish metallic spikes, the picture only improved. He followed the straps to perfectly rounded calves and the outline of tantalizing thighs lost in a skirt that moved when she did. The cream-colored skirt led to a sparkling gold top. Her shoulders were slight, the swells of her breasts snagging his attention for a beat, and her hair fell in curls over those small shoulders. Dark hair with a touch of mahogany, or maybe rich cherry. Not quite red, but with a notable amount of warmth.

HDEXP0619

He sipped from his glass, again taking in the skirt, both flirty and fun in equal measures. A guy could get lost in there. Get lost in her.

An inviting thought, indeed.

The brunette spun around, her skirt swirling, her smile a seemingly permanent feature. She was lively and vivid, and even in her muted gold-and-cream ensemble, somehow the brightest color in the room. A man approached her, and Reid promptly lost his smile, a strange feeling of propriety rolling over him and causing him to bristle.

The suited man was average height with a receding hairline. He was on the skinny side, but the vision in gold simply smiled up at him, dazzling the man like she'd cast a spell. When she shook her head in dismissal and the man ducked his head and moved on, relief swamped Reid, but he still didn't approach her.

Careful was the only way to proceed, or so instinct told him. She was open but somehow skittish, in an outfit he couldn't take his eyes from. He hadn't been in a rush to approach the goddess like some of the other men in the room.

Reid had already decided to carefully choose his moment, but as she made eye contact, he realized he wasn't going to have to approach her.

She was coming to him.

Don't miss a single book from

DYNASTIES

Secrets of the A-List

Available now!

Available now!

Available July 2019

And look out for

Redeemed by Passion

by Joss Wood

Coming August 2019!

Harlequin.com

HDBPA0619

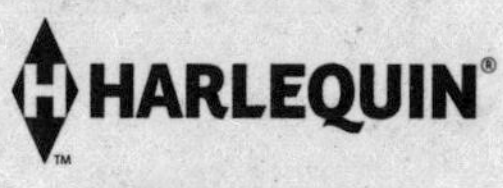
HARLEQUIN®